ELYSIA

Elysia checked out in all ways of preliminary survey—breathable atmosphere, climate within Earth limits and apparently less extreme; a water, oxygen and carbon dioxide life cycle; no unusual hazards. No signs of intelligent life. A watery world even more so than Terra, with over 90% oceans.

A good bet for colonization . . . or so they thought.

Then they met the natives!

───────────

"Rarely has Heinlein pushed his imagination further . . . a vivid, stirring experience."
—*Chicago Tribune*

Time for the Stars

Robert A. Heinlein

'A Del Rey Book

BALLANTINE BOOKS • NEW YORK

VL 7 & up
IL 7 & up

A Del Rey Book
Published by Ballantine Books

ISBN 0-345-32385-8

Printed in Canada

First Ballantine Books Edition: May 1978
Sixth Printing: October 1984

Cover art by Darrell K. Sweet

CONTENTS

I THE LONG RANGE FOUNDATION

According to their biographies, Destiny's favored children usually had their lives planned out from scratch. Napoleon was figuring on how to rule France when he was a barefoot boy in Corsica, Alexander the Great much the same, and Einstein was muttering equations in his cradle.

Maybe so. Me, I just muddled along.

In an old book that belonged to my great grandfather Lucas I once saw a cartoon of a man in evening clothes, going over a ski jump. With an expression of shocked unbelief he is saying: "How did I get up here?"

I know how he felt. How did I get 'way up here?

I was not even planned on. The untaxed quota for our family was three children, then my brother Pat and I came along in one giant economy package. We were a surprise to everyone, especially to my parents, my three sisters, and the tax adjusters. I don't recall being surprised myself but my earliest recollection is a vague feeling of not being quite welcome, even though Dad and Mum, and Faith, Hope, and Charity treated us okay.

Maybe Dad did not handle the emergency right. Many families get an extra child quota on an exchange basis with another family, or something, especially when the tax-free limit has already been filled with all boys or all girls. But Dad was stubborn, maintaining that the law was unconstitutional, unjust, discriminatory, against public morals, and contrary to the will of God. He could reel off a list of important people who were youngest children of large families,

7

from Benjamin Franklin to the first governor of Pluto, then he would demand to know where the human race would have been without them?—after which Mother would speak soothingly.

Dad was probably accurate as he was a student of almost everything, even his trade, which was micromechanics —but especially of history. He wanted to name us for his two heroes in American history, whereas Mother wanted to name us for her favorite artists. This is how I ended up as Thomas Paine Leonardo da Vinci Bartlett and my twin became Patrick Henry Michelangelo Bartlett. Dad called us Tom and Pat and Mother called us Leo and Michel and our sisters called us Useless and Double-Useless. Dad won by being stubborn.

Dad was stubborn. He could have paid the annual head tax on us supernumeraries, applied for a seven-person flat, and relaxed to the inevitable. Then he could have asked for reclassification. Instead he claimed exemption for us twins each year, always ended by paying our head tax with his check stamped "Paid under Protest!" and we seven lived in a five-person flat. When Pat and I were little we slept in homemade cribs in the bathroom which could not have been convenient for anybody, then when we were bigger we slept on the living-room couch, which was inconvenient for everybody, especially our sisters, who found it cramping to their social life.

Dad could have solved all this by putting in for family emigration to Mars or Venus, or the Jovian moons, and he used to bring up the subject. But this was the one thing that would make Mum more stubborn than he was. I don't know which part of making the High Jump scared her, because she would just settle her mouth and not answer. Dad would point out that big families got preferred treatment for emigration and that the head tax was earmarked to subsidize colonies off Earth and why shouldn't we benefit by the money we were being robbed of? To say nothing of letting our children grow up with freedom and elbow room, out where there wasn't a bureaucrat standing behind every

8

productive worker dreaming up more rules and restrictions? Answer me that?

Mother never answered and we never emigrated.

We were always short of money. Two extra mouths, extra taxes, and no family assistance for the two extras make the stabilized family income law as poor a fit as the clothes Mum cut down for us from Dad's old ones. It was darn' seldom that we could afford to dial for dinner like other people and Dad even used to bring home any of his lunch that he didn't eat. Mum went back to work as soon as we twins were in kindergarten, but the only household robot we had was an obsolete model "Morris Garage" *Mother's Helper* which was always burning out valves and took almost as long to program as the job would have taken. Pat and I got acquainted with dish water and detergents—at least I did; Pat usually insisted on doing the sterilizing or had a sore thumb or something.

Dad used to talk about the intangible benefits of being poor—learning to stand on your own feet, building character, and all that. By the time I was old enough to understand I was old enough to wish they weren't so intangible, but, thinking back, maybe he had a point. We did have fun. Pat and I raised hamsters in the service unit and Mum never objected. When we turned the bath into a chem lab the girls did make unfriendly comments but when Dad put his foot down, they sweet-talked him into picking it up again and after that they hung their laundry somewhere else, and later Mum stood between us and the house manager when we poured acid down the drain and did the plumbing no good.

The only time I can remember when Mum put her foot down was when her brother, Uncle Steve, came back from Mars and gave us some canal worms which we planned to raise and sell at a profit. But when Dad stepped on one in the shower (we had not discussed our plans with him) she made us give them to the zoo, except the one Dad had stepped on, which was useless. Shortly after that we ran away from home to join the High Marines—Uncle Steve was a ballistics sergeant—and when lying about our age did not work and they fetched us back, Mum not only did not scold us but had fed our snakes and our silkworms while we were gone.

Oh, I guess we were happy. It is hard to tell at the time. Pat and I were very close and did everything together but I want to get one thing straight: being a twin is not the Damon-and-Pythias dream that throb writers would have you think. It makes you close to another person to be born with him, share a room with him, eat with him, play with him, work with him, and hardly ever do anything without him as far back as you can remember, and farther according to witnesses. It makes you close; it makes you almost indispensable to each other—but it does not necessarily make you love him.

I want to get this straight because there has been a lot of nonsense talked about it since twins got to be suddenly important. I'm me; I'm not my brother Pat. I could always tell us apart, even if other people couldn't. He is the right-handed one; I'm the left-handed one. And from my point of view I'm the one who almost always got the small piece of cake.

I can remember times when he got both pieces through a fast shuffle. I'm not speaking in general; I'm thinking of a certain white cake with chocolate icing and how he confused things so that he got my piece, too, Mum and Dad thinking he was both of us, despite my protests. Dessert can be the high point of the day when you are eight, which was what we were then.

I am not complaining about these things . . . even though I feel a dull lump of anger even now, after all the years and miles, at the recollection of being punished because Dad and Mum thought I was the one who was trying to wangle two desserts. But I'm just trying to tell the truth. Doctor Devereaux said to write it all down and where I have to start is how it feels to be a twin. You aren't a twin, are you? Maybe you are but the chances are forty-four to one that you aren't —not even a fraternal, whereas Pat and I are identicals which is four times as unlikely.

They say that one twin is always retarded—I don't think

so. Pat and I were always as near alike as two shoes of a pair. The few times we showed any difference I was a quarter inch taller or a pound heavier, then we would even out. We got equally good marks in school; we cut our teeth together. What he did have was more grab than I had, something the psychologists call "pecking order." But it was so subtle you could not define it and other people could not see it. So far as I know, it started from nothing and grew into a pattern that neither of us could break even if we wanted to.

Maybe if the nurse had picked me up first when we were born *I* would have been the one who got the bigger piece of cake. Or maybe she did—I don't *know* how it started.

But don't think that being a twin is all bad even if you are on the short end; it is mostly good. You go into a crowd of strangers and you are scared and shy—and there is your twin a couple of feet away and you aren't alone any more. Or somebody punches you in the mouth and while you are groggy your twin has punched him and the fight goes your way. You flunk a quiz and your twin has flunked just as badly and you aren't alone.

But do not think that being twins is like having a very close and loyal friend. It isn't like that at all and it is a great deal closer.

Pat and I had our first contact with the Long Range Foundation when this Mr. Geeking showed up at our home. I did not warm to him. Dad didn't like him either and wanted to hustle him out, but he was already seated with coffee at his elbow for Mother's notions of hospitality were firm.

So this Geeking item was allowed to state his business. He was, he said, a field representative of "Genetics Investigations."

"What's that?" Dad said sharply.

" 'Genetics Investigations' is a scientific agency, Mr. Bartlett. This present project is one of gathering data concerning twins. It is in the public interest and we hope that you will cooperate."

Dad took a deep breath and hauled out the imaginary soapbox he always had ready. "More government meddling!

I'm a decent citizen; I pay my bills and support my family. My boys are just like other boys and I'm sick and tired of the government's attitude about them. I'm not going to have them poked and prodded and investigated to satisfy some bureaucrat. All we ask is to be left alone—and that the government admit the obvious fact that my boys have as much right to breathe air and occupy space as anyone else!"

Dad wasn't stupid; it was just that he had a reaction pattern where Pat and I were concerned as automatic as the snarl of a dog who has been kicked too often. Mr. Geeking tried to soothe him but Dad can't be interrupted when he has started that tape. "You tell the Department of Population Control that I'm not having their 'genetics investigations.' What do they want to find out? How to keep people from having twins, probably. What's wrong with twins? Where would Rome have been without Romulus and Remus? —answer me that! Mister, do you know how many—"

"*Please*, Mr. Bartlett, I'm not from the government."

"Eh? Well, why didn't you say so? Who are you from?"

"Genetics Investigations is an agency of the Long Range Foundation." I felt Pat's sudden interest. Everybody has heard of the Long Range Foundation, but it happened that Pat and I had just done a term paper on non-profit corporations and had used the Long Range Foundation as a type example.

We got interested in the purposes of the Long Range Foundation. Its coat of arms reads: "Bread Cast Upon the Waters," and its charter is headed: "Dedicated to the Welfare of Our Descendants." The charter goes on with a lot of lawyers' fog but the way the directors have interpreted it has been to spend money only on things that no government and no other corporation would touch. It wasn't enough for a proposed project to be interesting to science or socially desirable; it also had to be so horribly expensive that no one else would touch it and the prospective results had to lie so far in the future that it could not be justified to taxpayers or shareholders. To make the LRF directors light up with enthusiasm you had to suggest something that cost a billion or more and probably wouldn't show results for ten generations, if ever . . . something like how to control the weather (they're working on that) or where does your lap go when you stand up.

The funny thing is that bread cast upon waters does come back seven hundred fold; the most preposterous projects made the LRF embarrassing amounts of money—"embarrassing" to a non-profit corporation that is. Take space travel: it seemed tailor-made, back a couple of hundred years ago, for LRF, since it was fantastically expensive and offered no probable results comparable with the investment. There was a time when governments did some work on it for military reasons, but the Concord of Bayreuth in 1980 put a stop even to that.

So the Long Range Foundation stepped in and happily began wasting money. It came at a time when the corporation unfortunately had made a few billions on the Thompson mass-converter when they had expected to spend at least a century on pure research; since they could not declare a dividend (no stockholders), they had to get rid of the money somehow and space travel looked like a rat hole to pour it down.

Even the kids know what happened to that: Ortega's torch made space travel inside the solar system cheap, fast, and easy, and the one-way energy screen made colonization practical and profitable; the LRF could not unload fast enough to keep from making lots more money.

I did not think all this that evening; LRF was just something that Pat and I happened to know more about than most high school seniors . . . more than Dad knew, apparently, for he snorted and answered, "The Long Range Foundation, eh? I'd almost rather you were from the government. If boondoggles like that were properly taxed, the government wouldn't be squeezing head taxes out of its citizens."

This was not a fair statement, not a "flat-curve relationship," as they call it in Beginning Mathematical Empiricism. Mr. McKeefe had told us to estimate the influence, if any, of LRF on the technology "yeast-form" growth curve; either I should have flunked the course or LRF had kept the curve from leveling off early in the 21st century—I mean to say,

13

the "cultural inheritance," the accumulation of knowledge and wealth that keeps us from being savages, had increased greatly as a result of the tax-free status of such non-profit research corporations. I didn't dream up that opinion; there are figures to prove it. What would have happened if the tribal elders had forced Ugh to hunt with the rest of the tribe instead of staying home and whittling out the first wheel while the idea was bright in his mind?

Mr. Geeking answered, "I can't debate the merits of such matters, Mr. Bartlett. I'm merely an employee."

"And I'm paying your salary. Indirectly and unwillingly, but paying it nevertheless."

I wanted to get into the argument but I could feel Pat holding back. It did not matter; Mr. Geeking shrugged and said, "If so, I thank you. But all I came here for was to ask your twin boys to take a few tests and answer some questions. The tests are harmless and the results will be kept confidential."

"What are you trying to find out?"

I think Mr. Geeking was telling the truth when he answered, "I don't know. I'm merely a field agent; I'm not in charge of the project."

Pat cut in. "I don't see why not, Dad. Do you have the tests in your briefcase, Mr. Geeking?"

"Now, Patrick—"

"It's all right, Dad. Let's see the tests, Mr. Geeking."

"Uh, that's not what we had in mind. The Project has set up local offices in the TransLunar Building. The tests take about half a day."

"All the way downtown, huh, and a half day's time . . . what do you pay?"

"Eh? The subjects are asked to contribute their time in the interests of science."

Pat shook his head. "Sorry, Mr. Geeking. This is exam week . . . and my brother and I have part-time school jobs, too."

I kept quiet. Our exams were over, except Analysis of History, which is a snap course involving no math but statistics and pseudospatial calculus, and the school chem lab we worked in was closed for examinations. I was sure Dad did not know these things, or he would have butted in; Dad can shift from prejudice to being a Roman judge at the drop of a hint.

Pat stood up, so I stood up. Mr. Geeking sat tight. "Arrangements can be made," he said evenly.

Pat stuck him as much as we made for a month of washing bottles in the lab, just for one afternoon's work—then upped the ante when it was made clear that we would be obliged to take the tests together (as if we would have done it any other way!). Mr. Geeking paid without a quiver, in cash, in advance.

II THE NATURAL LOGARITHM
OF TWO

I never in my life saw so many twins as were waiting on the fortieth floor of the TransLunar Building the following Wednesday afternoon. I don't like to be around twins, they make me think I'm seeing double. Don't tell me I'm inconsistent; I *never* saw the twins I am part of—I just saw Pat.

Pat felt the same way; we had never been chummy with other twins. He looked around and whistled. "Tom, did you ever see such a mess of spare parts?"

"Never."

"If I were in charge, I'd shoot half of them." He hadn't spoken loud enough to offend anyone; Pat and I used a prison-yard whisper that no one else could hear although we never had trouble understanding it. "Depressing, isn't it?"

Then he whistled softly and I looked where he was looking. Twins of course, but this was a case of when once is good, twice is better. They were red-headed sisters, younger than we were but not too young—sixteen, maybe—and cute as Persian kittens.

Those sisters had the effect on us that a light has on a moth. Pat whispered, "Tom, we owe it to them to grant them a little of our time," and headed toward them, with me in step. They were dressed in fake Scottish outfits, green plaid which made their hair flame like bonfires and to us they looked as pretty as a new fall of snow.

And just as chilly. Pat got halfway through his opening speech when he trailed off and shut up; they were staring through him. I was blushing and the only thing that kept it from being a major embarrassing incident was a loud-speaker that commenced to bray:

"Attention, please! You are requested to report to the door marked with your surname initial." So we went to door A-to-D and the red-headed sisters headed toward the other end of the alphabet without ever having seen us at all. As we queued up Pat muttered, "Is there egg on my chin? Or have they taken a vow to be old maids?"

"Probably both," I answered. "Anyhow, I prefer blondes." This was true, since Maudie was a blonde. Pat and I had been dating Maudie Kauric for about a year—going steady you could call it, though in my case it usually meant that I was stuck with Maudie's chum Hedda Staley, whose notion of dazzling conversation was to ask me if I didn't think Maudie was the cutest thing ever? Since this was true and unanswerable, our talk did not sparkle.

"Well, so do I," Pat agreed, without saying which blonde —Maudie was the only subject on which we were reticent with each other. "But I have never had a closed mind." He shrugged and added cheerfully, "Anyhow, there are other possibilities."

There certainly were, for of the hundreds of twins present maybe a third were near enough our age not to be out of the question and half of them, as near as I could tell without counting, were of the sex that turns a mere crowd into a social event. However, none came up to the high standards of the redheads, so I began looking over the crowd as a whole.

The oldest pair I saw, two grown men, seemed to be not older than the early thirties and I saw one set of little girls about twelve—they had their mother in tow. But most of them were within a loud shout of twenty. I had concluded that "Genetics Investigations" was picking its samples by age groups when I found that we were at the head of the line and a clerk was saying, "Names, please?"

For the next two hours we were passed from one data collector to another, being fingerprinted, giving blood samples, checking "yes" or "no" to hundreds of silly questions that can't be answered "yes" or "no." The physical examination was thorough and involved the usual carefully planned nonsense of keeping a person standing in bare feet on a cold floor in a room five degrees too chilly for naked human skin while prodding the victim and asking him rude personal questions.

I was thoroughly bored and was not even amused when Pat whispered that we should strip the clothes off the doctor now and prod *him* in the belly and get the nurse to record how *he* liked it? My only pleasant thought was that Pat had stuck them plenty for their fun. Then they let us get dressed and ushered us into a room where a rather pretty woman sat behind a desk. She had a transparency viewer on her desk and was looking at two personality profiles superimposed on it. They almost matched and I tried to sneak a look to see where they did not. But I could not tell Pat's from my own and anyhow I'm not a mathematical psychologist.

She smiled and said, "Sit down, boys. I'm Doctor Arnault." She held up the profiles and a bunch of punched cards and added, "Perfect mirror twins, even to dextrocardia. This should be interesting."

Pat tried to look at the papers. "What's our I.Q. this time, Doctor?"

"Never mind." She put the papers down and covered them, then picked up a deck of cards. "Have you ever used these?"

Of course we had, for they were the classic Rhine test

cards, wiggles and stars and so forth. Every high school psychology class has a set and a high score almost always means that some bright boy has figured out a way to cold-deck the teacher. In fact Pat had worked out a simple way to cheat when our teacher, with a tired lack of anger, split us up and made us run tests only with other people—whereupon our scores dropped to the limits of standard error. So I was already certain that Pat and I weren't ESP freaks and the Rhine cards were just another boring test.

But I could feel Pat become attentive. "Keep your ears open, kid," I heard him whisper, "and we'll make this interesting." Dr. Arnault did not hear him, of course.

I wasn't sure we ought to but I knew if he could manage to signal to me I would not be able to refrain from fudging the results. But I need not have worried; Dr. Arnault took Pat out and returned without him. She was hooked by microphone to the other test room but there was no chance to whisper through it; it was hot only when she switched it on.

She started right in. "First test run in twenty seconds, Mabel," she said into the mike and switched it off, then turned to me. "Look at the cards as I turn them," she said. "Don't try, don't strain. Just look at them."

So I looked at the cards. This went on with variations for maybe an hour. Sometimes I was supposed to be receiving, sometimes sending. As far as I was concerned nothing happened, for they never told us our scores.

Finally Dr. Arnault looked at a score sheet and said, "Tom, I want to give you a mild injection. It won't hurt you and it'll wear off before you go home. Okay?"

"What sort?" I said suspiciously.

"Don't fret; it is harmless. I don't want to tell you or you might unconsciously show the reaction you expected."

"Uh, what does my brother say? Does he get one, too?"

"Never mind, please. I'm asking you."

I still hesitated. Dad did not favor injections and such unless necessary; he had made a fuss over our taking part in the encephalitis program. "Are you an M.D.?" I asked.

"No, my degree is in science. Why?"

"Then how do you know it's harmless?"

She bit her lip, then answered, "I'll send for a doctor of medicine, if you prefer."

"Uh, no, I guess that won't be necessary." I was remembering something that Dad had said about the sleeping sickness shots and I added, "Does the Long Range Foundation carry liability insurance for this?"

"What? Why, I think so. Yes, I'm sure they do." She looked at me and added, "Tom, how does a boy your age get to be so suspicious?"

"Huh? Why ask me? You're the psychologist, ma'am. Anyhow," I added, "if you had sat on as many tacks as I have, you'd be suspicious too."

"Mmm . . . never mind. I've been studying for years and I still don't know what the younger generation is coming to. Well, are you going to take the injection?"

"Uh, I'll take it—since the LRF carries insurance. Just write out what it is you are giving me and sign it."

She got two bright pink spots in her cheeks. But she took out stationery, wrote on it, folded it into an envelope and sealed it. "Put it in your pocket," she said briskly. "Don't look at it until the experiments are over. Now bare your left forearm."

As she gave me the shot she said sweetly, "This is going to sting a little . . . I hope." It did.

She turned out all the lights except the light in the transparency viewer. "Are you comfortable?"

"Sure."

"I'm sorry if I seemed vexed. I want you to relax and be comfortable." She came over and did something to the chair I was in; it opened out gently until I was practically lying in a hammock. "Relax and don't fight it. If you find yourself getting sleepy, that is to be expected." She sat down and all I could see was her face, illuminated by the viewer. She was awfully pretty, I decided, even though she was too old for it to matter . . . at least thirty, maybe older. And she was nice, too. She spoke for a few minutes in her gentle voice but I don't remember exactly what she said.

I must have gone to sleep, for next it was pitch dark and Pat was right there by me, although I hadn't noticed the light go out nor the door being opened. I started to speak when I heard him whisper:

"*Tom, did you ever see such nonsensical rigamarole?*"

I whispered back, "Reminds me of the time we were initiated into the Congo Cannibals."

"*Keep your voice down; they'll catch on.*"

"You're the one who is talking too loud. Anyhow, who cares? Let's give 'em the Cannibal war whoop and scare 'em out of their shoes."

"*Later, later. Right now my girl friend Mabel wants me to give you a string of numbers. So we'll let them have their fun first. After all, they're paying for it.*"

"Okay."

"*Point six nine three one.*"

"That's the natural logarithm of two."

"*What did you think it was? Mabel's telephone number? Shut up and listen. Just repeat the numbers back. Three point one four five nine . . .*"

It went on quite a while. Some were familiar numbers like the first two; the rest may have been random or even Mabel's phone number, for all of me. I got bored and was beginning to think about sticking in a war whoop on my own when Dr. Arnault said quietly, "End of test run. Both of you please keep quiet and relax for a few minutes. Mabel, I'll meet you in the data comparison room." I heard her go out, so I dropped the war whoop notion and relaxed. Repeating all those numbers in the dark had made me dopey anyhow—and as Uncle Steve says, when you get a chance to rest, do so; you may not get another chance soon.

Presently I heard the door open again, then I was blinking at bright lights. Dr. Arnault said, "That's all today, Tom . . . and thank you very much. We want to see you and your brother at the same time tomorrow."

I blinked again and looked around. "Where's Pat? What does he say?"

"You'll find him in the outer lobby. He told me that you could come tomorrow. You can, can't you?"

"Uh, I suppose so, if it's all right with him." I was feeling sheepish about the trick we had pulled, so I added, "Dr. Arnault? I'm sorry I annoyed you."

She patted my hand and smiled. "That's all right. You were right to be cautious and you were a good subject. You should see the wild ones we sometimes draw. See you tomorrow."

Pat was waiting in the big room where we had seen the redheads. He fell into step and we headed for the drop. "I raised the fee for tomorrow," he whispered smugly.

"You did? Pat, do you think we should do this? I mean, fun is fun, but if they ever twig that we are faking, they'll be sore. They might even make us pay back what they've already paid us."

"How can they? We've been paid to show up and take tests. We've done that. It's up to them to rig tests that can't be beaten. I could, if I were doing it."

"Pat, you're dishonest and crooked, both." I thought about Dr. Arnault . . . she was a nice lady. "I think I'll stay home tomorrow."

I said this just as Pat stepped off the drop. He was ten feet below me all the way down and had forty stories in which to consider his answer. As I landed beside him he answered by changing the subject. "They gave you a hypodermic?"

"Yes."

"Did you think to make them sign an admission of liability, or did you goof?"

"Well, sort of." I felt in my pocket for the envelope; I'd forgotten about it. "I made Dr. Arnault write down what she was giving us."

Pat reached for the envelope. "My apologies, maestro. With my brains and your luck we've got them where we want them." He started to open the envelope. "I bet it was neopentothal—or one of the barbiturates."

I snatched it back. "That's mine."

"Well, open it," he answered, "and don't obstruct traffic. I want to see what dream drug they gave us."

We had come out into the pedestrian level and his advice did have merit. Before opening it I led us across the change strips onto the fast-west strip and stepped behind a wind break. As I unfolded the paper Pat read over my shoulder:

" 'Long Range Fumbling, and so forth—injections given to subjects 7L435 & -6 T. P. Bartlett & P. H. Bartlett (iden-twins)—each one-tenth c.c. distilled water raised to normal salinity,' signed 'Doris Arnault, Sc.D., for the Foundation.' Tom, we've been hoaxed!"

I stared at it, trying to fit what I had experienced with what the paper said. Pat added hopefully, "Or is this the hoax? Were we injected with something else and they didn't want to admit it?"

"No," I said slowly. I was sure Dr. Arnault wouldn't write down "water" and actually give us one of the sleeping drugs—she wasn't that sort of person. "Pat, we weren't drugged . . . we were *hypnotized.*"

He shook his head. "Impossible. Granting that I could be hypnotized, you couldn't be. Nothing there to hypnotize. And I wasn't hypnotized, comrade. No spinning lights, no passes with the hands—why, my girl Mabel didn't even stare in my eyes. She just gave me the shot and told me to take it easy and let it take effect."

"Don't be juvenile, Pat. Spinning lights and such is for suckers. I don't care whether you call it hypnotism or sales-manship. They gave us hypos and suggested that we would be sleepy—so we fell asleep."

"So I was sleepy! Anyhow that wasn't quite what Mabel did. She told me not to go to sleep, or if I did, to wake up when she called me. Then when they brought you in, she—"

"Wait a minute. You mean when they moved you back into the room I was in—"

"No, I don't mean anything of the sort. After they brought you in, Mabel gave me this list of numbers and I read them to you and—"

"Wait a minute," I said. "Pat, you're mixed up. How could you *read* them in pitch darkness? She must have read them to you. I mean—" I stopped, for I was getting mixed up myself. Well, she could have read to him from another room. "Were you wearing headphones?"

"What's that got to do with it? Anyhow, it wasn't pitch dark, not after they brought you in. She held up the numbers on a board that was rigged with a light of its own, enough to let me see the numbers and her hands."

"Pat, I wish you wouldn't keep repeating nonsense. Hypnotized or not, I was never so dopey that I couldn't notice anything that happened. I was never moved anywhere; they probably wheeled you in without disturbing you. And the room we were in was pitch dark, not a glimmer."

Pat did not answer right away, which wasn't like him. At last he said, "Tom, are you sure?"

"Sure I'm sure!"

He sighed. "I hate to say this, because I know what you will say. But what are you supposed to do when none of your theories fits?"

"Huh? Is this a quiz? You throw 'em away and try a new one. Basic methodology, freshman year."

"Okay, just slip this on for size, don't mind the pattern: Tom, my boy, brace yourself—we're *mind* readers."

I tried it and did not like it. "Pat, just because you can't explain everything is no reason to talk like the fat old women who go to fortune tellers. We're muddled, I admit, whether it was drugs or hypnosis. But we couldn't have been reading each other's minds or we would have been doing it years ago. We would have noticed."

"Not necessarily. There's never anything much going on in your mind, so why should I notice?"

"But it stands to reason—"

"What's the natural log of two?"

" 'Point six nine three one' is what you said, though I've got very little use for four-place tables. What's that got to do with it?"

"I used four-place because she gave it to me that way. Do you remember what she said just before I gave you that number?"

"Huh? Who?"

"Mabel. Dr. Mabel Lichtenstein. What did she say?"

"Nobody said anything."

"Tom, my senile symbiote, she told me what to do, to wit, read the numbers to you. She told me this in a clear, penetrating soprano. You didn't hear her?"

"No."

"Then you weren't in the same room. You weren't within earshot, even though I was prepared to swear that they had shoved you in right by me. I *knew* you were there. But you weren't. So it was telepathy."

I was confused. I didn't feel telepathic; I merely felt hungry.

"Me, too, on both counts," Pat agreed. "So let's stop at Berkeley Station and get a sandwich."

I followed him off the strips, feeling not quite as hungry and even more confused. Pat had answered a remark I had not made.

III PROJECT LEBENSRAUM

Even though I was told to take my time and tell everything, it can't be done. I haven't had time to add to this for days, but even if I didn't have to work I still could not "tell all," because it takes *more* than a day to write down what happens in one day. The harder you try the farther behind you get. So I'm going to quit trying and just hit the high spots.

Anyhow everybody knows the general outline of Project Lebensraum.

We did not say anything to Mum and Dad about that first day. You can't expose parents to that sort of thing; they get jittery and start issuing edicts. We just told them the tests would run a second day and that nobody had told us what the results were.

Dr. Arnault seemed unsurprised when we told her we

knew the score, even when I blurted out that we thought we had been faking but apparently weren't. She just nodded and said that it had been necessary to encourage us to think that everything was commonplace, even if there had to be a little fibbing on both sides. "I had the advantage of having your personality analyses to guide me," she added. "Sometimes in psychology you have to go roundabout to arrive at the truth.

"We'll try a more direct way today," she went on. "We'll put you two back to back but close enough together that you unquestionably can hear each other. But I am going to use a sound screen to cut you off partly or completely from time to time without your knowing it."

It was a lot harder the second time. Naturally we tried and naturally we flubbed. But Dr. Arnault was patient and so was Dr. Lichtenstein—Pat's "Dr. Mabel." She preferred to be called Dr. Mabel; she was short and pudgy and younger than Dr. Arnault and about as cute as a female can be and still look like a sofa pillow. It wasn't until later that we found out she was boss of the research team and world famous. "Giggly little fat girl" was an act she used to put ordinary people, meaning Pat and myself, at their ease. I guess this proves you should ignore the package and read the fine print.

So she giggled and Dr. Arnault looked serious and we could not tell whether we were reading minds or not. I could hear Tom's whispers—they told us to go ahead and whisper —and he could hear mine and sometimes they would fade. I was sure we weren't getting anything, not telepathy I mean, for it was just the way Pat and I used to whisper answers back and forth in school without getting caught.

Finally Dr. Mabel giggled sheepishly and said, "I guess that's enough for today. Don't you think so, Doctor?"

Dr. Arnault agreed and Pat and I sat up and faced each other. I said, "I suppose yesterday was a fluke. I guess we disappointed you."

Dr. Mabel looked like a startled kitten. Dr. Arnault answered soberly, "I don't know what you expected, Tom, but for the past hour you and your brother have been cut off from hearing each other during every test run."

"But I *did* hear him."

"You certainly did. But not with your ears. We've been recording each side of the sound barrier. Perhaps we should play back part of it."

Dr. Mabel giggled. "That's a good idea." So they did. It started out with all four voices while they told us what they wanted, then there were just my whispers and Pat's, reading lines back and forth from *The Comedy of Errors*. They must have had parabolic mikes focused on us for our whispers sounded like a wind storm.

Pat's whispers gradually faded out. But mine kept right on going . . . answering a dead silence.

We signed a research contract with the Foundation and Dad countersigned it, after an argument. He thought mind-reading was folderol and we did not dispute him, since the clincher was that money was scarce as always and it was a better-paying job than any summer job we could get, fat enough to insure that we could start college even if our scholarships didn't come through.

But before the summer was over they let us in on the connection between "Genetics Investigations" and "Project Lebensraum." That was a horse of another color—a very dark black, from our parents' standpoint.

Long before that time Pat and I could telepath as easily as we could talk and just as accurately, without special nursing and at any distance. We must have been doing it for years without knowing it—in fact Dr. Arnault made a surprise recording of our prison-yard whispering (when we weren't trying to telepath, just our ordinary private conversation) and proved that neither one of us could understand our recorded whispers when we were keeping it down low to keep other people from hearing.

She told us that it was theoretically possible that everyone was potentially telepathic, but that it had proved difficult to demonstrate it except with identical twins—and then only with about ten per cent. "We don't know why, but think of an analogy with tuned radio circuits."

PROJECT LEBENSRAUM

"Brain waves?" I asked.

"Don't push the analogy too far. It can't be the brain waves we detect with an encephalograph equipment or we would have been selling commercial telepathic equipment long since. And the human brain is not a radio. But whatever it is, two persons from the same egg stand an enormously better chance of being 'tuned in' than two non-twins do. I can't read your mind and you can't read mine and perhaps we never will. There have been only a few cases in all the history of psychology of people who appeared to be able to 'tune in' on just anyone, and most of those aren't well documented."

Pat grinned and winked at Dr. Mabel. "So we are a couple of freaks."

She looked wide-eyed and started to answer but Dr. Arnault beat her to it. "Not at all, Pat. In you it is normal. But we do have teams in the project who are not identical twins. Some husbands and wives, a few fraternal siblings, even some pairs who were brought together by the research itself. They are the 'freaks.' If we could find out how *they* do it, we might be able to set up conditions to let anyone do it."

Dr. Mabel shivered. "What a terrible thought! There is too little privacy now."

I repeated this to Maudie (with Pat's interruptions and corrections)—because the news services had found out what was going on in "Genetics Investigations" and naturally we "mind readers" came in for a lot of silly publicity and just as naturally, under Hedda Staley's mush-headed prodding, Maudie began to wonder if a girl had any privacy? She had, of course; I could not have read her mind with a search warrant, nor could Pat. She would have believed our simple statement if Hedda had not harped on it. She nearly managed to bust us up with Maudie, but we jettisoned her instead and we had threesome dates with Maudie until Pat was sent away.

But that wasn't until nearly the end of the summer after they explained Project Lebensraum.

About a week before our contract was to run out they

27

gathered us twins together to talk to us. There had been enough to crowd a big conference room by the end of hundreds that first day, dozens the second day, but just summer. The redheads were among the survivors but Pat and I did not sit by them even though there was room; they still maintained their icicle attitude and were self-centered as oysters. The rest of us were all old friends by now.

A Mr. Howard was introduced as representing the Foundation. He ladled out the usual guff about being happy to meet us and appreciating the honor and so forth. Pat said to me. *"Hang onto your wallet, Tom. This bloke is selling something."* Now that we knew what we were doing Pat and I talked in the presence of other people, even more than we used to. We no longer bothered to whisper since we had proved to us that we weren't hearing the whispers. But we did subvocalize the words silently, as it helped in being understood. Early in the summer we had tried to do without words and read minds directly but it did not work. Oh, I could latch on to Pat, but the silly, incoherent rumbling that went on in his mind in place of thought was confusing and annoying, as senseless as finding yourself inside another person's dream. So I learned not to listen unless he "spoke" to me and he did the same. When we did, we used words and sentences like anybody else. There was none of this fantastic, impossible popular nonsense about instantly grasping the contents of another person's mind; we simply "talked."

One thing that had bothered me was why Pat's telepathic "voice" sounded like his real one. It had not worried me when I did not know what we were doing, but once I realized that these "sounds" weren't sounds, it bothered me. I began to wonder if I was all there and for a week I could not "hear" him—psychosomatic telepathic-deafness Dr. Arnault called it.

She got me straightened out by explaining what hearing is. You don't hear with your ears, you hear with your brain; you don't see with your eyes, you see with your brain. When you touch something, the sensation is not in your finger, it is inside your head. The ears and eyes and fingers are just data collectors; it is the brain that abstracts order out of a chaos

28

of data and gives it meaning. "A new baby does not really see," she said. "Watch the eyes of one and you can see that it doesn't. Its eyes work but its brain has not yet learned to see. But once the brain has acquired the habits of abstracting as 'seeing' and 'hearing,' the habit persists. How would you expect to 'hear' what your twin says to you telepathically? As little tinkling bells or dancing lights? Not at all. You expect words, your brain 'hears' words; it is a process it is used to and knows how to handle."

I no longer worried about it. I could hear Pat's voice clearer than I could hear the voice of the speaker addressing us. No doubt there were fifty other conversations around us, but I heard no one but Pat and it was obvious that the speaker could not hear anybody (and that he did not know much about telepathy) for he went on:

"Possibly a lot of you wonderful people—" (This with a sickening smile) "—are reading my mind right now. I hope not, or if you are I hope you will bear with me until I have said my say."

"What did I tell you?" Pat put in. *"Don't sign anything until I check it."*

("Shut up,") I told him. ("I want to listen.") His voice used to sound like a whisper; now it tended to drown out real sounds.

Mr. Howard went on, "Perhaps you have wondered why the Long Range Foundation has sponsored this research. The Foundation is always interested in anything which will add to human knowledge. But there is a much more important reason, a supremely important reason . . . and a grand purpose to which you yourselves can be supremely important."

"See? Be sure to count your change."

("Quiet, Pat.")

"Let me quote," Mr. Howard continued, "from the charter of the Long Range Foundation: 'Dedicated to the welfare of our descendants.' " He paused dramatically—I think that was what he intended. "Ladies and gentlemen, what one thing above all is necessary for our descendants?"

"Ancestors!" Pat answered promptly. For a second I

29

thought that he had used his vocal cords. But nobody else noticed.

"There can be only one answer—living room! Room to grow, room to raise families, broad acres of fertile grain, room for parks and schools and homes. We have over five billion human souls on this planet; it was crowded to the point of marginal starvation more than a century ago with only half that number. Yet this afternoon there are a quarter of a million more of us than there were at this same hour yesterday —ninety million more people each year. Only by monumental efforts of reclamation and conservation, plus population control measures that grow daily more difficult, have we been able to stave off starvation. We have placed a sea in the Sahara, we have melted the Greenland ice cap, we have watered the windy steppes, yet each year there is more and more pressure for more and more room for endlessly more people."

I don't care for orations and this was all old stuff. Shucks, Pat and I knew it if anyone did; we were the kittens that should have been drowned; our old man paid a yearly fine for our very existence.

"It has been a century since the inception of interplanetary travel; man has spread through the Solar System. One would think that nine planets would be ample for a race too fertile for one. Yet you all know that such has not been the case. Of the daughters of Father Sol only fair Terra is truly suited to Man."

"I'll bet he writes advertising slogans."

("Poor ones,") I agreed.

"Colonize the others we have done, but only at a great cost. The sturdy Dutch in pushing back the sea have not faced such grim and nearly hopeless tasks as the colonists of Mars and Venus and Ganymede. What the human race needs and must have are not these frozen or burning or airless discards of creation. We need more planets like this gentle one we are standing on. And there *are* more, many more!" He waved his hands at the ceiling and looked up. "There are dozens, hundreds, thousands, countless hordes of them . . . out there. Ladies and gentlemen, *it is time for the stars!*"

"*Here comes the pitch,*" Pat said quietly. "*A fast curve, breaking inside.*"

("Pat, what the deuce is he driving at?")

"*He's a real estate agent.*"

Pat was not far off but I am not going to quote the rest of Mr. Howard's speech. He was a good sort when we got to know him but he was dazzled by the sound of his own voice, so I'll summarize. He reminded us that the Torchship *Avant-Garde* had headed out to Proxima Centauri six years back. Pat and I knew about it not only from the news but because mother's brother, Uncle Steve, had put in for it—he was turned down, but for a while we enjoyed prestige just from being related to somebody on the list—I guess we gave the impression around school that Uncle Steve was certain to be chosen.

Nobody had heard from the *Avant-Garde* and maybe she would be back in fifteen or twenty years and maybe not. The reason we hadn't heard from her, as Mr. Howard pointed out and everybody knows, is that you don't send radio messages back from a ship light-years away and traveling just under the speed of light. Even if you assumed that a ship could carry a power plant big enough to punch radio messages across light-years (which may not be impossible in some cosmic sense but surely is impossible in terms of modern engineering)—even so, what use are messages which travel just barely faster than the ship that sends them? The *Avant-Garde* would be home almost as quickly as any report she could send, even by radio.

Some fuzzbrain asked about messenger rockets. Mr. Howard looked pained and tried to answer and I didn't listen. If radio isn't fast enough, how can a messenger rocket be faster? I'll bet Dr. Einstein spun in his grave.

Mr. Howard hurried on before there were any more silly interruptions. The Long Range Foundation proposed to send out a dozen more starships in all directions to explore Sol-type solar systems for Earth-type planets, planets for colonization. The ships might be gone a long time, for each one would explore more than one solar system.

"And this, ladies and gentlemen, is where you are indispensable to this great project for living room—for *you* will be the means whereby the captains of those ships report back what they have found!"

Even Pat kept quiet.

Presently a man stood up in the back of the room. He was one of the oldest twins among us; he and his brother were about thirty-five. "Excuse me, Mr. Howard, but may I ask a question?"

"Surely."

"I am Gregory Graham; this is my brother Grant Graham. We're physicists. Now we don't claim to be expert in cosmic phenomena but we do know something about communication theory. Granting for the sake of argument that telepathy would work over interstellar distances—I don't think so but I've no proof that it wouldn't—even granting that, I can't see where it helps. Telepathy, light, radio waves, even gravity, are all limited to the speed of light. That is in the very nature of the physical universe, an ultimate limit for all communication. Any other view falls into the ancient philosophical contradiction of action-at-a-distance. It is just possible that you might use telepathy to report findings and let the ship go on to new explorations—but the message would still take light-years to come back. Communication back and forth between a starship and Earth, even by telepathy, is utterly impossible, contrary to the known laws of physics." He looked apologetic and sat down.

I thought Graham had him on the hip. Pat and I got good marks in physics and what Graham had said was the straight word, right out of the book. But Howard did not seem bothered. "I'll let an expert answer. Dr. Lichtenstein? If you please—"

Dr. Mabel stood up and blushed and giggled and looked flustered and said, "I'm terribly sorry, Mr. Graham, I really am, but telepathy isn't like that at all." She giggled again and said, "I shouldn't be saying this, since you are telepathic and I'm not, but telepathy doesn't pay the least bit of attention to the speed of light."

"But it *has* to. The laws of physics—"

"Oh, dear! Have we given you the impression that telepathy is physical?" She twisted her hands. "It probably isn't."

"Everything is physical. I include 'physiological,' of course."

"It is? You do? Oh, I wish I could be sure . . . but physics has always been much too deep for me. But I don't know how you can be sure that telepathy is physical; we haven't been able to make it register on any instrument. Dear me, we don't even know how consciousness hooks into matter. Is consciousness physical? I'm sure I don't know. But we do know that telepathy is faster than light because we measured it."

Pat sat up with a jerk. *"Stick around, kid. I think we'll stay for the second show."*

Graham looked stunned. Dr. Mabel said hastily, "I didn't do it; it was Dr. Abernathy."

"Horatio Abernathy?" demanded Graham.

"Yes, that's his first name, though I never dared call him by it. He's rather important."

"Just the Nobel prize," Graham said grimly, "in field theory. Go on. What did he find?"

"Well, we sent this one twin out to Ganymede—such an awfully long way. Then we used simultaneous radio-telephony and telepathy messages, with the twin on Ganymede talking by radio while he was talking directly—telepathically, I mean—to his twin back in Buenos Aires. The telepathic message always beat the radio message by about forty minutes. That would be right, wouldn't it? You can see the exact figures in my office."

Graham managed to close his mouth. "When did this happen? Why hasn't it been published? Who has been keeping it secret? It's the most important thing since the Michelson-Morley experiment—it's terrible!"

Dr. Mabel looked upset and Mr. Howard butted in soothingly. "Nobody has been suppressing knowledge, Mr. Graham, and Dr. Abernathy is preparing an article for publication in the *Physical Review.* However I admit that the

Foundation did ask him not to give out an advance release in order to give us time to go ahead with another project —the one you know as 'Genetics Investigations'—on a crash-priority basis. We felt we were entitled to search out and attempt to sign up potential telepathic teams before every psychological laboratory and, for that matter, every ambitious showman, tried to beat us to it. Dr. Abernathy was willing—he doesn't like premature publication."

"If it will make you feel better, Mr. Graham," Dr. Mabel said diffidently, "telepathy doesn't pay attention to the inverse-square law either. The signal strength was as strong at half a billion miles as when the paired telepaths were in adjoining rooms."

Graham sat down heavily. "I don't know whether it does or it doesn't. I'm busy rearranging everything I have ever believed."

The interruption by the Graham brothers had explained some things but had pulled us away from the purpose of the meeting, which was for Mr. Howard to sell us on signing up as spacemen. He did not have to sell me. I guess every boy wants to go out into space; Pat and I had run away from home once to enlist in the High Marines—and this was much more than just getting on the Earth-Mars-Venus run; this meant exploring the stars.

The Stars!

"We've told you about this before your research contracts run out," Mr. Howard explained, "so that you will have time to consider it, time for us to explain the conditions and advantages."

I did not care what the advantages were. If they had invited me to hook a sled on behind, I would have said yes, not worrying about torch blast or space suits or anything.

"Both members of each telepathic team will be equally well taken care of," he assured us. "The starside member will have good pay and good working conditions in the finest of modern torchships in the company of crews selected for psychological compatibility as well as for special training; the earthside member will have his financial future assured, as well as his physical welfare." He smiled. "Most assuredly his physical welfare, for it is necessary that he be kept alive and well as long as science can keep him so. It is not too much to say that signing this contract will add thirty years to your lives."

It burst on me why the twins they had tested had been young people. The twin who went out to the stars would not age very much, not at the speed of light. Even if he stayed away a century it would not seem that long to him—but his twin who stayed behind would grow older. They would have to pamper him like royalty, keep him alive—or their "radio" would break down.

Pat said, *"Milky Way, here I come!"*

But Mr. Howard was still talking. "We want you to think this over carefully; it is the most important decision you will ever make. On the shoulders of you few and others like you in other cities around the globe, all told just a tiny fraction of one per cent of the human race, on you precious few rest the hopes of all humanity. So think carefully and give us a chance to explain anything which may trouble you. Don't act hastily."

The red-headed twins got up and walked out, noses in the air. They did not have to speak to make it clear that they would have nothing to do with anything so unladylike, so rude and crude, as exploring space. In the silence in which they paraded out Pat said to me, *"There go the Pioneer Mothers. That's the spirit that discovered America."* As they passed us he cut loose with a loud razzberry—and I suddenly realized that he was not telepathing when the redheads stiffened and hurried faster. There was an embarrassed laugh and Mr. Howard quickly picked up the business at hand as if nothing had happened while I bawled Pat out.

Mr. Howard asked us to come back at the usual time tomorrow, when Foundation representatives would explain details. He invited us to bring our lawyers, or (those of us who were under age, which was more than half) our parents and their lawyers.

Pat was bubbling over as we left, but I had lost my enthusiasm. In the middle of Mr. Howard's speech I had had a great light dawn: one of us was going to have to stay behind and I knew as certainly as bread falls butter side down which one it would be. A possible thirty more years on my life was no inducement to me. What use is thirty extra years wrapped in cottonwool? There would be no spacing for the twin left behind, not even inside the Solar System . . . and I had never even been to the Moon.

I tried to butt in on Pat's enthusiasm and put it to him fair and square, for I was darned if I was going to take the small piece of cake this time without argument.

"Look, Pat, I'll draw straws with you for it. Or match coins."

"Huh? What are you talking about?"

"You know what I'm talking about!"

He just brushed it aside and grinned. "You worry too much, Tom. They'll pick the teams the way they want to. It won't be up to us."

I knew he was determined to go and I knew I would lose.

IV HALF A LOAF

Our parents made the predictable uproar. A conference in the Bartlett family always sounded like a zoo at feeding time but this one set a new high. In addition to Pat and myself, Faith, Hope, and Charity, and our parents, there was Faith's fairly new husband, Frank Dubois, and Hope's brand-new fiancé, Lothar Sembrich. The last two did not count and both of them seemed to me to be examples of what lengths a girl will go to in order to get married, but they used up space and occasionally contributed remarks to confuse the issue. But Mother's brother, Uncle Steve, was there, too, having popped up on Earthside furlough.

It was Uncle Steve's presence that decided Pat to bring it out in the open instead of waiting to tackle Dad and Mum one at a time. Both of them considered Unce Steve a disturbing influence but they were proud of him; one of his rare visits was always a holiday.

Mr. Howard had given us a sample contract to take home and look over. After dinner Pat said, "By the way, Dad, the Foundation offered us a new contract today, a long-term one." He took it out of his pocket but did not offer it to Dad.

"I trust you told them that you were about to start school again?"

"Sure, we told them that, but they insisted that we take the contract home to show our parents. Okay, we knew what your answer would be." Pat started to put the contract into his pocket.

I said to Pat privately, ("What's the silly idea? You've made him say 'no' and now he can't back down.")

"Not yet he hasn't," Pat answered on our private circuit. *"Don't joggle my elbow."*

Dad was already reaching out a hand. "Let me see it. You should never make up your mind without knowing the facts."

Pat was not quick about passing it over. "Well, there *is* a scholarship clause," he admitted, "but Tom and I wouldn't be able to go to school together the way we always have."

"That's not necessarily bad. You two are too dependent on each other. Some day you will have to face the cold, cruel world alone . . . and going to different schools might be a good place to start."

Pat stuck out the contract, folded to the second page, "It's paragraph ten."

Dad read paragraph ten first, just as Pat meant him to do, and his eyebrows went up. Paragraph ten agreed that the party of the first part, the LRF, would keep the party of the second part in any school of his choice, all expenses, for the duration of the contract, or a shorter time at his option, and agreed to do the same for the party of the third part after the completion of the active period of the contract, plus tutoring during the active period—all of which was a long-winded way of saying that the Foundation would put the one who stayed home through school now and the one who went starside through school when he got back . . . all this in addition to our salaries; see paragraph seven.

So Dad turned to paragraph seven and his eyebrows went higher and his pipe went out. He looked at Pat. "Do I understand that they intend to appoint you two 'communications technicians tenth grade' with no experience?"

Uncle Steve sat up and almost knocked his chair over. "Bruce, did you say 'tenth grade'?"

"So it says."

"Regular LRF pay scales?"

"Yes. I don't know how much that is, but I believe they ordinarily hire skilled ratings beginning at third grade."

Uncle Steve whistled. "I'd hate to tell you how much money it is, Bruce—but the chief electron pusher on Pluto is tenth pay grade . . . and it took him twenty years and a doctor's degree to get there." Uncle Steve looked at us. "Give out, shipmates. Where did they bury the body? Is it a bribe?" Pat did not answer. Uncle Steve turned to Dad and said, "Never mind the fine print, Bruce; just have the kids sign it. Each one of them will make more than you and me together. Never argue with Santa Claus."

But Dad was already reading the fine print, from subparagraph one-A to the penalty clauses. It was written in lawyer language but what it did was to sign us up as crew members for one voyage of an LRF ship, except that one of us was required to perform his duties Earthside. There was lots more to nail it down so that the one who stayed Earthside could not wiggle out, but that was all it amounted to.

The contract did not say where the ship would go or how long the voyage would last.

Dad finally put the contract down and Charity grabbed it. Dad took it from her and passed it over to Mother. Then he said, "Boys, this contract looks so favorable that I suspect there must be a catch. Tomorrow morning I'm going to get hold of Judge Holland and ask him to go over it with me. But if I read it correctly, you are being offered all these benefits—and an extravagant salary—provided one of you makes one voyage in the *Lewis and Clark*."

Uncle Steve said suddenly, "The *Lewis and Clark*, Bruce?"

"The *Lewis and Clark*, or such sister ship as may be designated. Why? You know the ship, Steve?"

Uncle Steve got poker-faced and answered, "I've never been in her. New ship, I understand. Well equipped."

"I'm glad to hear it." Dad looked at Mum. "Well, Molly?"

Mother did not answer. She was reading the contract and steadily getting whiter. Uncle Steve caught my eye and shook his head very slightly. I said to Pat, ("Uncle Steve has spotted the catch in it.")

"He won't hinder."

Mother looked up at last and spoke to Dad in a high voice. "I suppose you are going to consent?" She sounded sick. She put down the contract and Charity grabbed it again just as Hope grabbed it from the other side. It ended with our brother-in-law Frank Dubois holding it while everybody else read over his shoulders.

"Now, my dear," Dad said mildly, "remember that boys do grow up. I would like to keep the family together forever—but it can't be that way and you know it."

"Bruce, you promised that they would not go out into space."

Her brother shot her a glance—his chest was covered with ribbons he had won in space. But Dad went on just as mildly. "Not quite, dear. I promised you that I would not consent to minority enlistment in the peace forces; I want them to finish school and I did not want you upset. But this is another matter . . . and, if we refuse, it won't be long before they can enlist whether we like it or not."

Mother turned to Uncle Steve and said bitterly, "Stephen, you put this idea in their heads."

He looked annoyed then answered as gently as Dad. "Take it easy, Sis. I've been away; you can't pin this on me. Anyhow, you don't put ideas in boys' heads; they grow them naturally."

Frank Dubois cleared his throat and said loudly, "Since this seems to be a family conference, no doubt you would like my opinion."

I said, to Pat only, ("Nobody asked your opinion, you lard head!")

Pat answered, *"Let him talk. He's our secret weapon, maybe."*

"If you want the considered judgment of an experienced businessman, this so-called contract is either a practical joke or a proposition so preposterous as to be treated with contempt. I understand that the twins are supposed to have some freak talent—although I've seen no evidence of it—but the idea of paying them more than a man receives in his mature years, well, it's just not the right way to raise boys. If they were sons of mine, I would forbid it. Of course, they're not—"

"No, they're not," Dad agreed.

Frank looked sharply at him. "Was that sarcasm, Father Bartlett? I'm merely trying to help. But as I told you the other day, if the twins will go to some good business school and work hard, I'd find a place for them in the bakery. If they make good, there is no reason why they should not do as well as I have done." Frank was his father's junior partner in an automated bakery; he always managed to let people know how much money he made. "But as for this notion of going out into space, I've always said that if a man expects to make anything of himself, he should stay home and work. Excuse me, Steve."

Uncle Steve said woodenly, "I'd be glad to excuse you."

"Eh?"

"Forget it, forget it. You stay out of space and I'll promise not to bake any bread. By the way, there's flour on your lapel."

Frank glanced down hastily. Faith brushed at his jacket and said, "Why, that's just powder."

"Of course it is," Frank agreed, brushing at it himself. "I'll have you know, Steve, that I'm usually much too busy to go down on the processing floor. I'm hardly ever out of the office."

"So I suspected."

Frank decided that he and Faith were late for another appointment and got up to go, when Dad stopped them. "Frank? What was that about my boys being freaks?"

"What? I never said anything of the sort."

"I'm glad to hear it."

They left in a sticky silence, except that Pat was humming silently and loudly the *March of the Gladiators*. *"We've got it won, kid!"*

It seemed so to me, too—but Pat had to press our luck. He picked up the contract. "Then it's okay, Dad?"

"Mmm . . . I want to consult Judge Holland—and I'm not speaking for your mother." That did not worry us; Mum wouldn't hold out if Dad agreed, especially not with Uncle Steve around. "But you could say that the matter has not been disapproved." He frowned. "By the way, there is no time limit mentioned in there."

Uncle Steve fielded that one for us. "That's customary on a commercial ship, Bruce . . . which is what this is, legally. You sign on for the voyage, home planet to home planet."

"Uh, no doubt. But didn't they give you some idea, boys?"

I heard Pat moan, *"There goes the ball game. What'll we tell him, Tom?"* Dad waited and Uncle Steve eyed us.

Finally Uncle Steve said, "Better speak up, boys. Perhaps I should have mentioned that I'm trying to get a billet on one of those ships myself—special discharge and such. So I know."

Pat muttered something. Dad said sharply, "Speak up, son."

"They told us the voyage would probably last . . . about a century."

Mum fainted and Uncle Steve caught her and everybody rushed around with cold compresses getting in each other's way and we were all upset. Once she pulled out of it Uncle Steve said to Dad, "Bruce? I'm going to take the boys out and buy them a tall, strong sarsaparilla and get them out from under foot. You won't want to talk tonight anyhow."

Dad agreed absently that it was a good idea. I guess

Dad loved all of us; nevertheless, when the chips were down, nobody counted but Mother.

Uncle Steve took us to a place where he could get something more to his taste than sarsaparilla, then vetoed it when Pat tried to order beer. "Don't try to show off, youngster. You are not going to put me in the position of serving liquor to my sister's kids."

"Beer can't hurt you."

"So? I'm still looking for the bloke who told me it was a soft drink. I'm going to beat him to a pulp with a stein. Pipe down." So we picked soft drinks and he drank some horrible mixture he called a Martian shandy and we talked about Project Lebensraum. He knew more about it than we did even though no press release had been made until that day—I suppose the fact that he had been assigned to the Chief of Staff's office had something to do with it, but he did not say.

Presently Pat looked worried and said, "See here, Uncle Steve, is there any chance that they will let us? Or should Tom and I just forget it?"

"Eh? Of course they are going to let you do it."

"Huh? It didn't look like it tonight. If I know Dad, he would skin us for rugs rather than make Mum unhappy."

"No doubt. And a good idea. But believe me, boys, this is in the bag . . . provided you use the right arguments."

"Which is?"

"Mmm . . . boys, being a staff rating, I've served with a lot of high brass. When you are right and a general is wrong, there is only one way to get him to change his mind. You shut up and don't argue. You let the facts speak for themselves and give him time to figure out a logical reason for reversing himself."

Pat looked unconvinced; Uncle Steve went on, "Believe me. Your pop is a reasonable man and, while your mother is not, she would rather be hurt herself than make anybody she loves unhappy. That contract is all in your favor and they can't refuse—provided you give them time to adjust to the idea. But if you tease and bulldoze and argue the way you usually do, you'll get them united against you."

HALF A LOAF

"Huh? But I never tease, I merely use logical—"

"Stow it, you make me tired. Pat, you were one of the most unlovable brats that ever squawled to get his own way . . . and, Tom, you weren't any better. You haven't mellowed with age; you've simply sharpened your techniques. Now you are being offered something free that I would give my right arm to have. I ought to stand aside and let you flub it. But I won't. Keep your flapping mouths shut, play this easy, and it's yours. Try your usual loathsome tactics and you lose."

We would not take that sort of talk from most people. Anybody else and Pat would have given me the signal and he'd 've hit him high while I hit him low. But you don't argue that way with a man who wears the Ceres ribbon; you listen. Pat didn't even mutter to me about it.

So we talked about Project Lebensraum itself. Twelve ships were to go out, radiating from Sol approximately in axes of a duodecahedron—but only approximately, as each ship's mission would be, not to search a volume of space, but to visit as many Sol-type stars as possible in the shortest time. Uncle Steve explained how they worked out a "minimax" search curve for each ship but I did not understand it; it involved a type of calculus we had not studied. Not that it mattered; each ship was to spend as much time exploring and as little time making the jumps as possible.

But Pat could not keep from coming back to the idea of how to sell the deal to our parents. "Uncle Steve? Granting that you are right about playing it easy, here's an argument that maybe they should hear? Maybe you could use it on them?"

"Um?"

"Well, if half a loaf is better than none, maybe they haven't realized that this way one of us stays home." I caught a phrase of what Pat had started to say, which was not "one of us stays home," but "Tom stays home." I started to object, then let it ride. He hadn't said it. Pat went on, "They know we want to space. If they don't let us do this, we'll do it any way we can. If we joined your corps, we might come home on leave—but not often. If we emigrate, we might as

43

well be dead; very few emigrants make enough to afford a trip back to Earth, not while their parents are still alive, at least. So if they keep us home now, as soon as we are of age they probably will never see us again. But if they agree, not only does one stay home, but they are always in touch with the other one—that's the whole purpose in using us telepath pairs." Pat looked anxiously at Uncle Steve. "Shouldn't we point that out? Or will you slip them the idea?"

Uncle Steve did not answer right away, although I could not see anything wrong with the logic. Two from two leaves zero, but one from two still leaves one.

Finally he answered slowly, "Pat, can't you get it through your thick head to leave well enough alone?"

"I don't see what's wrong with my logic."

"Since when was an emotional argument won by logic? You should read about the time King Solomon proposed to divvy up the baby." He took a pull at his glass and wiped his mouth. "What I am about to tell you is strictly confidential. Did you know that the Planetary League considered commissioning these ships as warships?"

"Huh? Why? Mr. Howard didn't say—"

"Keep your voice down. Project Lebensraum is of supreme interest to the Department of Peace. When it comes down to it, the root cause of war is always population pressure no matter what other factors enter in."

"But we've abolished war."

"So we have. So chaps like me get paid to stomp out brush fires before they burn the whole forest. Boys, if I tell you the rest of this, you've *got* to keep it to yourselves now and forever."

I don't like secrets. I'd rather owe money. You can't pay back a secret. But we promised.

"Okay. I saw the estimates the Department of Peace made on this project at the request of LRF. When the *Avant-Garde* was sent out, they gave her one chance in nine of returning. We've got better equipment now; they figure one chance in six for each planetary system visited. Each ship visits an average of six stars on the schedule laid out—so each ship has one chance in thirty-six of coming back. For twelve ships that means one chance in three of maybe *one* ship coming back. That's where you freaks come in."

"Don't call us 'freaks'!" We answered together.

" 'Freaks,' " he repeated. "And everybody is mighty glad you freaks are around, because without you the thing is impossible. Ships and crews are expendable—ships are just money and they can always find people like me with more curiosity than sense to man the ships. But while the ships are expendable, the knowledge they will gather is not expendable. Nobody at the top expects these ships to come back—but we've *got* to locate those earth-type planets; the human race needs them. That is what you boys are for: to report back. Then it won't matter that the ships won't come back."

"I'm not scared," I said firmly.

Pat glanced at me and looked away. I hadn't telepathed but I had told him plainly that the matter was not settled as to which one of us would go. Uncle Steve looked at me soberly and said, "I didn't expect you to be, at your age. Nor am I; I've been living on borrowed time since I was nineteen. By now I'm so convinced of my own luck that if one ship comes back, I'm sure it will be mine. But do you see why it would be silly to argue with your mother that half a set of twins is better than none? Emotionally your argument is all wrong. Go read the Parable of the Lost Sheep. You point out to your mother that one of you will be safe at home and it will simply fix her mind on the fact that the other one *isn't* safe and *isn't* home. If your Pop tries to reassure her, he is likely to stumble onto these facts—for they aren't secret, not the facts on which the statisticians based their predictions; it is just that the publicity about this project will emphasize the positive and play down the negative."

"Uncle Steve," objected Pat, "I don't see how they can be sure that most of the ships will be lost."

"They can't be sure. But these are actually optimistic assumptions based on what experience the race has had with investigating strange places. It's like this, Pat: you can be right over and over again, but when it comes to exploring strange places, the first time you guess wrong is the last guess you make. You're dead. Ever looked at the figures about it in just this one tiny solar system? Exploration is like Russian roulette; you can win and win, but if you keep on, it will kill you, certain. So don't get your parents stirred up on this phase of the matter. *I* don't mind—a man is entitled to die the way he wants to; that's one thing they haven't taxed. But there is no use in drawing attention to the fact that one of you two isn't coming back."

V THE PARTY OF THE SECOND PART

Uncle Steve was right about the folks giving in; Pat left for the training course three weeks later.

I still don't know just how it was that Pat got to be the one. We never matched for it, we never had a knock-down argument, and I never agreed. But Pat went.

I tried to settle it with him several times but he always put me off, telling me not to worry and to wait and see how things worked out. Presently I found it taken for granted that Pat was going and I was staying. Maybe I should have made a stand the day we signed the contract, when Pat hung back and let me sign first, thereby getting me down on paper as the party of the second part who stayed home, instead of party of the third part who went. But it had not seemed worth making a row about, as the two were interchangeable by agreement among the three parties to the contract. Pat pointed this out to me just before we signed; the important thing was to get the contract signed while our parents were holding still—get *their* signatures.

Was Pat trying to put one over on me right then? If so, I didn't catch him wording his thoughts. Contrariwise, would I have tried the same thing on him if I had thought of it? I don't know, I just don't know. In any case, I gradually became aware that the matter was settled; the family took it for granted and so did the LRF people. So I told Pat it was *not* settled. He just shrugged and reminded me that it had not been his doing. Maybe I could get them to change their minds . . . if I didn't care whether or not I upset the apple-cart.

I didn't want to do that. We did not know that the LRF would have got down on its knees and wept rather than let any young and healthy telepath pair get away from them; we thought they had plenty to choose from. I thought that if I made a fuss they might tear up the contract, which they could do up till D-Day by paying a small penalty.

Instead I got Dad alone and talked to him. This shows how desperate I was; neither Pat nor I ever went alone to our parents about the other one. I didn't feel easy about it, but stammered and stuttered and had trouble making Dad understand why I felt swindled.

Dad looked troubled and said, "Tom, I thought you and your brother had settled this between you?"

"That's what I'm trying to tell you! We didn't."

"What do you expect me to do?"

"Why, I want you to make him be fair about it. We ought to match for it, or something. Or you could do it for us and keep it fair and square. Would you?"

Dad gave attention to his pipe the way he does when he is stalling. At last he said, "Tom, I don't see how you can back out now, after everything is settled. Unless you want me to break the contract? It wouldn't be easy but I can."

"But I don't have to break the contract. I just want an even chance. If I lose, I'll shut up. If I win, it won't change anything—except that I would go and Pat would stay."

"Mmm . . ." Dad puffed on his pipe and looked thoughtful. "Tom, have you looked at your mother lately?"

I had, but I hadn't talked with her much. She was moving around like a zombie, looking grief-stricken and hurt. "Why?"

"I can't do this to her. She's already going through the agony of losing your brother; I can't put her through it on your account, too. She couldn't stand it."

I knew she was feeling bad, but I could not see what difference it would make if we swapped. "You're not suggesting that Mum wants it this way? That she would rather have Pat go than me?"

"I am not. Your mother loves you both, equally."

"Then it would be just the same to her."

"It would not. She's undergoing the grief of losing one of her sons. If you swapped now, she would have to go through it afresh for her other son. That wouldn't be fair." He knocked his pipe against an ash tray, which was the same as gaveling that the meeting was adjourned. "No, son, I'm afraid that you will just have to stand by your agreement."

It was hopeless so I shut up. With Dad, bringing Mum's welfare into it was the same as trumping an ace.

Pat left for the training center four days later. I didn't see much of him except the hours we spent down at the Trans-Lunar Building for he was dating Maudie every night and I was not included. He pointed out that this was the last he would see of her whereas I would have plenty of time—so get lost, please. I did not argue; it was not only fair, taken by itself, but I did not want to go along on their dates under the circumstances. Pat and I were farther apart those last few days than we had ever been.

It did not affect our telepathic ability, however, whatever this "tuning" was that some minds could do went right on and we could do it as easily as we could talk . . . and turn it off as easily, too. We didn't have to "concentrate" or "clear our minds" or any of that Eastern mysticism nonsense. When we wanted to "talk," we talked.

When Pat left I felt lost. Sure, I was in touch with him four hours a day and any other time I cared to call him, but you can't live your whole life doing things by two's without getting out of joint when you have to do things by one's. I didn't have new habits yet. I'd get ready to go someplace, then I would stop at the door and wonder what I had forgotten. Just Pat. It is mighty lonesome to start off somewhere by yourself when you've always done it with someone.

Besides that, Mum was being brightly cheerful and tender and downright unbearable, and my sleep was all broken up. The training center worked on Switzerland's time zone which meant that I, and all other twins who were staying behind no matter where on Earth they were, worked our practice messages on Swiss time, too. Pat would whistle in my ears and wake me at two in the morning each night and then I would work until dawn and try to catch up on sleep in the daytime.

It was inconvenient but necessary and I was well paid. For the first time in my life I had plenty of money. So did all of our family, for I started paying a fat board bill despite Dad's objections. I even bought myself a watch (Pat had taken ours with him) without worrying about the price, and we were talking about moving into a bigger place.

But the LRF was crowding more and more into my life and I began to realize that the contract covered more than just recording messages from my twin. The geriatrics program started at once. "Geriatrics" is a funny term to use about a person not old enough to vote but it had the special meaning here of making me live as long as possible by starting on me at once. What I ate was no longer my business; I had to follow the diet they ordered, no more sandwiches picked up casually. There was a long list of "special hazard" things I must not do. They gave me shots for everything from housemaid's knee to parrot fever and I had a physical examination so thorough as to make every other one seem like a mere laying on of hands.

The only consolation was that Pat told me they were doing the same to him. We might be common as mud most ways but we were irreplaceable communication equipment to LRF, so we got the treatment a prize race horse or a prime minister gets and which common people hardly ever get. It was a nuisance.

I did not call Maudie the first week or ten days after Pat left; I didn't feel easy about her. Finally she called me and asked if I were angry with her or was she in quarantine? So we made a date for that night. It was not festive. She called me "Pat" a couple of times, which she used to do every now and then and it had never mattered, since Pat and I were used to people mixing up our names. But now it was awkward, because Pat's ghost was a skeleton at the feast.

The second time she did it I said angrily, "If you want to talk to Pat, I can get in touch with him in half a second!"

"What? Why, Tom!"

"Oh, I know you would rather I was Pat! If you think I enjoy being second choice, think again."

She got tears in her eyes and I got ashamed and more difficult. So we had a bitter argument and then I was telling her how I had been swindled.

Her reaction wasn't what I expected. Instead of sympathy she said, "Oh, Tom, Tom! Can't you see that Pat didn't do this to you? You did it to yourself."

"Huh?"

"It's not his fault; it's your own. I used to get so tired of the way you let him push you around. You *liked* having him push you around. You've got a 'will to fail.' "

I was so angry I had trouble answering. "What are you talking about? That sounds like a lot of cheap, chimney-corner psychiatry to me. Next thing you know you'll be telling me I have a 'death wish.' "

She blinked back tears. "No. Maybe Pat has that. He was always kidding about it but, just the same, I know how dangerous it is. I know we won't see him again."

I chewed that over. "Are you trying to say," I said slowly, "that I let Pat do me out of it because I was afraid to go?"

"What? Why, Tom dear, I never said anything of the sort."

"It sounded like it." Then I knew why it sounded like it. Maybe I *was* afraid. Maybe I had struggled just hard enough to let Pat win . . . because I knew what was going to happen to the one who went.

Maybe I was a coward.

We made it up and the date seemed about to end satisfactorily. When I took her home I was thinking of trying to kiss her good night—I never had, what with the way Pat and I were always in each other's hair. I think she expected me to, too . . . when Pat suddenly whistled at me.

"Hey! You awake, mate?"

("Certainly,") I answered shortly. ("But I'm busy.")

"How busy? Are you out with my girl?"

("What makes you think that?")

"You are, aren't you? I figured you were. How are you making out?"

("Mind your own business!")

"Sure, sure! Just say hello to her for me. Hi, Maudie!"

Maudie said, "Tom, what are you so preoccupied about?"

I answered, "Oh, it's just Pat. He says to say hello to you."

"Oh . . . well, hello to him from me."

So I did. Pat chuckled. *"Kiss her good night for me."*

So I didn't, not for either of us.

But I called her again the next day and we went out together regularly after that. Things began to be awfully pleasant where Maudie was concerned . . . so pleasant that I even thought about the fact that college students sometimes got married and now I would be able to afford it, if it happened to work out that way. Oh, I wasn't dead sure I wanted to tie myself down so young, but it is mighty lonely to be alone when you've always had somebody with you.

Then they brought Pat home on a shutter.

It was actually an ambulance craft, specially chartered. The idiot had sneaked off and tried skiing, which he knew as much about as I know about pearl diving. He did not have much of a tumble; he practically fell over his own feet. But there he was, being carried into our flat on a stretcher, numb from the waist down and his legs useless. He should have been taken to a hospital, but he wanted to come home and Mum wanted him to come home, so Dad insisted on it. He wound up in the room Faith had vacated and I went back to sleeping on the couch.

The household was all upset, worse than it had been when Pat went away. Dad almost threw Frank Dubois out of the house when Frank said that now that this space travel nonsense was disposed of, he was still prepared to give Pat a job if he would study bookkeeping, since a bookkeeper could work from a wheelchair. I don't know; maybe Frank had good intentions, but I sometimes think "good intentions" should be declared a capital crime.

But the thing that made me downright queasy was the way Mother took it. She was full of tears and sympathy and she could not do enough for Pat—she spent hours rubbing his legs, until she was ready to collapse. But I could see, even if Dad couldn't, that she was indecently happy—she had her "baby" back. Oh, the tears weren't fake . . . but females seem able to cry and be happy at the same time.

We all knew that the "space travel nonsense" was washed up, but we did not discuss it, not even Pat and I; while he was flat on his back and helpless and no doubt feeling even worse than I did was no time to blame him for hogging things and then wasting our chance. Maybe I was bitter but it was no time to let him know. I was uneasily aware that the fat LRF checks would stop soon and the family would be short of money again when we needed it most and I regretted that expensive watch and the money I had blown in taking Maudie to places we had never been able to afford, but I avoided thinking about even that; it was spilt milk. But I did wonder what kind of a job I could get instead of starting college.

I was taken off guard when Mr. Howard showed up—I had halfway expected that LRF would carry us on the payroll until after Pat was operated on, even though the accident was not their fault and was the result of Pat's not obeying their regulations. But with the heaps of money they had I thought they might be generous.

But Mr. Howard did not even raise the question of the Foundation paying for, or not paying for, Pat's disability; he simply wanted to know how soon I would be ready to report to the training center?

I was confused and Mother was hysterical and Dad was angry and Mr. Howard was bland. To listen to him you would have thought that nothing had happened, certainly nothing which involved the slightest idea of letting us out of our contract. The parties of the second part and of the third part were interchangeable; since Pat could not go, naturally I would. Nothing had happened which interfered with our efficiency as a communication team. To be sure, they had let us have a few days to quiet down in view of the sad accident—but could I report at once? Time was short.

Dad got purple and almost incoherent. Hadn't they done enough to his family? Didn't they have any decency? Any consideration?

In the middle of it, while I was trying to adjust to the new situation and wondering what I should say, Pat called me silently. *"Tom! Come here!"*

I excused myself and hurried to him. Pat and I had hardly telepathed at all since he had been hurt. A few times he had called me in the night to fetch him a drink of water or something like that, but we had never really talked, either out loud or in our minds. There was just this black, moody silence that shut me out. I didn't know how to cope with it; it was the first time either of us had ever been ill without the other one.

But when he called I hurried in. "Shut the door."

I did so. He looked at me grimly. "I caught you before you promised anything, didn't I?"

"Yeah."

"Go out there and tell Dad I want to see him right away. Tell Mum I asked her to please quit crying, because she is getting me upset." He smiled sardonically. "Tell Mr. Howard to let me speak to my parents alone. Then you beat it."

"Huh?"

"Get out, don't stop to say good-by and don't say where you are going. When I want you, I'll tell you. If you hang around, Mother will work on you and get you to promise things." He looked at me bleakly. "You never did have any will power."

I let the dig slide off; he was ill. "Look, Pat, you're up against a combination this time. Mother is going to get her own way no matter what and Dad is so stirred up that I'm surprised he hasn't taken a poke at Mr. Howard."

"I'll handle Mother, and Dad, too. Howard should have stayed away. Get going. Split 'em up, then get lost."

"All right," I said uneasily. "Uh . . . look, Pat, I appreciate this."

He looked at me and his lip curled. "Think I'm doing this for you?"

"Why, I thought—"

"You never think . . . and I've been doing nothing else for days. If I'm going to be a cripple, do you fancy I'm going to spend my life in a public ward? Or here, with Mother drooling over me and Dad pinching pennies and the girls getting sick of the sight of me? Not Patrick! If I have to be like this, I'm going to have the best of everything . . . nurses to jump when I lift a finger and dancing girls to entertain me—and you are going to see that the LRF pays for it. We can keep our contract and we're going to. Oh, I know you don't want to go, but now you've *got* to."

"Me? You're all mixed up. You crowded me out. You—"

"Okay, forget it. You're rarin' to go." He reached up and punched me in the ribs, then grinned. "So we'll both go—for you'll take me along every step of the way. Now get out there and break that up."

I left two days later. When Pat handed Mum his reverse-twist whammie, she did not even fight. If getting the money to let her sick baby have proper care and everything else he wanted meant that I had to space, well, it was too bad but that was how it was. She told me how much it hurt to have me go but I knew she was not too upset. But *I* was, rather . . . I wondered what the score would have been if it had been *I* who was in Pat's fix? Would she have let Pat go just as easily simply to get *me* anything I wanted? But I decided to stop thinking about it; parents probably don't know that they are playing favorites even when they are doing it.

Dad got me alone for a man-to-man talk just before I left. He hemmed and hawed and stuck in apologies about how he should have talked things over with me before this and seemed even more embarrassed than I was, which was plenty. When he was floundering I let him know that one of our high school courses had covered most of what he was trying to say. (I didn't let him know that the course had been an anti-climax.) He brightened up and said, "Well, son, your mother and I have tried to teach you right from wrong. Just remember that you are a Bartlett and you won't make too many mistakes. On that other matter, well, if you will always ask yourself whether a girl is the sort you would be proud to bring home to meet your mother, I'll be satisfied."

I promised—it occurred to me that I wasn't going to have much chance to fall into bad company, not with psychologists practically dissecting everybody in Project Lebensraum. The bad apples were never going into the barrel.

When I see how naïve parents are I wonder how the human race keeps on being born. Just the same it was touching and I appreciate the ordeal he put himself through to get me squared away—Dad was always a decent guy and meant well.

I had a last date with Maudie but it wasn't much; we spent it sitting around Pat's bed. She did kiss me good-by—Pat told her to. Oh, well!

VI TORCHSHIP "LEWIS AND CLARK"

I was in Switzerland only two days. I got a quick look at the lake at Zurich and that was all; the time was jammed with trying to hurry me through all the things Pat had been studying for weeks. It couldn't be done, so they gave me spools of minitape which I was to study after the trip started.

I had one advantage: Planetary League Auxiliary Speech

was a required freshman course at our high school—P-L lingo was the working language of Project Lebensraum. I can't say I could speak it when I got there, but it isn't hard. Oh, it seems a little silly to say "goed" when you've always said "gone" but you get used to it, and of course all technical words are Geneva-International and always have been.

Actually, as subproject officer Professor Brunn pointed out, there was not a lot that a telepathic communicator had to know before going aboard ship; the principal purpose of the training center had been to get the crews together, let them eat and live together, so that the psychologists could spot personality frictions which had not been detected through tests.

"There isn't any doubt about you, son. We have your brother's record and we know how close your tests come to matching his. You telepaths have to deviate widely from accepted standards before we would disqualify one of you."

"Sir?"

"Don't you see? We can turn down a ship's captain just for low blood sugar before breakfast and a latent tendency to be short tempered therefrom until he has had his morning porridge. We can fill most billets twenty times over and juggle them until they are matched like a team of acrobats. But not you people. You are so scarce that we must allow you any eccentricity which won't endanger the ship. I wouldn't mind if you believed in astrology—you don't, do you?"

"Goodness, no!" I answered, shocked.

"You see? You're a normal, intelligent boy; you'll do. Why, we would take your twin, on a stretcher, if we had to."

Only telepaths were left when I got to Zurich. The captains and the astrogation and torch crews had joined the ships first, and then the specialists and staff people. All the "idlers" were aboard but us. And I hardly had time to get acquainted even with my fellow mind readers.

They were an odd bunch and I began to see what Professor Brunn meant by saying that we freaks had to be allowed a little leeway. There were a dozen of us—just for the

Lewis and Clark, I mean; there were a hundred and fifty for the twelve ships of the fleet, which was every telepathic pair that LRF had been able to sign up. I asked one of them, Bernhard van Houten, why each ship was going to carry so many telepaths?

He looked at me pityingly. "Use your head, Tom. If a radio burns out a valve, what do you do?"

"Why, you replace it."

"There's your answer. We're spare parts. If either end of a telepair dies or anything, that 'radio' is burned out, permanently. So they plug in another one of us. They want to be sure they have at least one telepair still working right up to the end of the trip . . . they hope."

I hardly had time to learn their names before we were whisked away. There was myself and Bernhard van Houten, a Chinese-Peruvian girl named Mei-Ling Jones (only she pronounced it "Hone-Ace"), Rupert Hauptman, Anna Horoshen, Gloria Maria Antonita Docampo, Sam Rojas, and Prudence Mathews. These were more or less my age. Then there was Dusty Rhodes who looked twelve and claimed to be fourteen. I wondered how LRF had persuaded his parents to permit such a child to go. Maybe they hated him; it would have been easy to do.

Then there were three who were older than the rest of us: Miss Gamma Furtney, Cas Warner, and Alfred McNeil. Miss Gamma was a weirdie, the sort of old maid who never admits to more than thirty; she was our triplet. LRF had scraped up four sets of triplets who were m-r's and could be persuaded to go; they were going to be used to tie the twelve ships together into four groups of three, then the groups could be hooked with four sets of twins.

Since triplets are eighty-six times as scarce as twins it was surprising that they could find enough who were telepathic and would go, without worrying about whether or not they were weirdies. I suspect that the Misses Alpha, Beta, and Gamma Furtney were attracted by the Einstein time effect; they could get even with all the men who had not married them by not getting older while those men died of old age.

We were a "corner" ship and Cas Warner was our sidewise twin, who would hook us through his twin to the *Vasco da Gama*, thus linking two groups of three. Other sidewise twins tied the other corners. The ones who worked ship-to-ship did not have to be young, since their twins (or triplets) were not left back on Earth, to grow older while their brothers or sisters stayed young through relativity. Cas Warner was forty-five, a nice quiet chap who seemed to enjoy eating with us kids.

The twelfth was Mr. ("Call me 'Uncle Alfred' ") McNeil, and he was an old darling. He was a Negro, his age was anything from sixty-five on up (I couldn't guess), and he had the saintliness that old people get when they don't turn sour and self-centered instead . . . to look at him you would bet heavy odds that he was a deacon in his church.

I got acquainted with him because I was terribly home-sick the first night I was in Zurich and he noticed it and invited me to his room after supper and sort of soothed me. I thought he was one of the Foundation psychologists, like Professor Brunn—but no, he was half of a telepair himself . . . and not even a sidewise twin; his partner was staying on Earth.

I couldn't believe it until he showed me a picture of his pair partner—a little girl with merry eyes and pigtails—and I finally got it through my thick head that here was that rarity, a telepathic pair who were not twins. She was Celestine Regina Johnson, his great-niece—only he called her "Sugar Pie" after he introduced me to the photograph and had told her who I was.

I had to pause and tell Pat about it, not remembering that he had already met them.

Uncle Alfred was retired and had been playmate-in-chief to his baby great-niece, for he had lived with his niece and her husband. He had taught the baby to talk. When her parents were both killed in an accident he had gone back to work rather than let the child be adopted. "I found out that I could keep tabs on Sugar Pie even when I couldn't see her. She was always a good baby and it meant I could watch out for her even when I had to be away. I knew it was a gift; I figured that the Lord in His infinite mercy had granted what I needed to let me take care of my little one."

The only thing that had worried him was that he might not live long enough, or, worse still, not be able to work long enough, to permit him to bring up Sugar Pie and get her started right. Then Project Lebensraum had solved everything. No, he didn't mind being away from her because he was *not* away from her; he was with her every minute.

I gathered an impression that he could actually see her but I didn't want to ask. In any case, with him stone walls did not a prison make nor light-years a separation. He knew that the Infinite Mercy that had kept them together this long would keep them together long enough for him to finish his appointed task. What happened after that was up to the Lord.

I had never met anybody who was so quietly, serenely happy. I didn't feel homesick again until I left him and went to bed. So I called Pat and told him about getting acquainted with Uncle Alfred. He said sure, Uncle Alf was a sweet old codger . . . and now I should shut up and go to sleep, as I had a hard day ahead of me tomorrow.

Then they zoomed us out to the South Pacific and we spent one night on Canton Atoll before we went aboard. They wouldn't let us swim in the lagoon even though Sam had arranged a picnic party of me and himself and Mei-Ling and Gloria; swimming was one of the unnecessary hazards. Instead we went to bed early and were awakened two hours before dawn—a ghastly time of day, particularly when your time sense has been badgered by crossing too many time zones too fast. I began to wonder what I was doing there and why?

The *Lewis and Clark* was a few hundred miles east of there in an unused part of the ocean. I had not realized how much water there was until I took a look at it from the air—and at that you see just the top. If they could figure some way to use all those wet acres as thoroughly as they use the Mississippi Valley they wouldn't need other planets.

From the air the *Lewis and Clark* looked like a basketball floating in water; you could not see that it was really shaped like a turnip. It floated with the torch down; the hemispherical upper part was all that showed. I got one look at her, with submersible freighters around her looking tiny in comparison, then our bus was hovering over her and we were being told to mind our step on the ladder and not leave anything behind in the bus. It occurred to me that it wouldn't do any good to write to Lost-and-Found if we did. It was a chilly thought . . . I guess I was still homesick, but mostly I was excited.

I got lost a couple of times and finally found my stateroom just as the speaker system was booming: "All hands, prepare for acceleration. Idlers strap down. Boost stations report in order. Minus fourteen minutes." The man talking was so matter of fact that he might as well have been saying, "Local passengers change at Birmingham."

The stateroom was big enough, with a double wardrobe and a desk with a built-in viewer-recorder and a little washstand and two pull-down beds. They were down, which limited the floor space. Nobody else was around so I picked one, lay down and fastened the three safety belts. I had just done so when that little runt Dusty Rhodes stuck his head in. "Hey! You got my bed!"

I started to tell him off, then decided that just before boost was no time for an argument. "Suit yourself," I answered, unstrapped, and moved into the other one, strapped down again.

Dusty looked annoyed; I think he wanted an argument. Instead of climbing into the one I had vacated, he stuck his head out the door and looked around. I said, "Better strap down. They already passed the word."

"Tripe," he answered without turning. "There's plenty of time. I'll take a quick look in the control room."

I was going to suggest that he go outside while he was about it when a ship's officer came through, checking the rooms. "In you get, son," he said briskly, using the no-nonsense tone in which you tell a dog to heel. Dusty opened his mouth, closed it, and climbed in. Then the officer "baby-strapped" him, pulling the buckles around so that they could not be reached by the person in the bunk. He even put the chest strap around Dusty's arms.

He then checked my belts. I had my arms outside the straps but all he said was, "Keep your arms on the mattress during boost," and left.

A female voice said, "All special communicators link with your telepartners."

I had been checking with Pat ever since I woke up and had described the *Lewis and Clark* to him when we first sighted her and then inside as well. Nevertheless I said, ("Are you there, Pat?")

"Naturally. I'm not going anyplace. What's the word?"

("Boost in about ten minutes. They just told us to link with our partners during boost.")

"You had better stay linked, or I'll beat your ears off! I don't want to miss anything."

("Okay, okay, don't race your engine. Pat? This isn't quite the way I thought it would be.")

"Huh? How?"

("I don't know. I guess I expected brass bands and speeches and such. After all, this is a big day. But aside from pictures they took of us last night at Canton Atoll, there was more fuss made when we started for Scout camp.")

Pat chuckled. *"Brass bands would get wet where you are —not to mention soaked with neutrons."*

("Sure, sure.") I didn't have to be told that a torchship needs elbow room for a boost. Even when they perfected a way to let them make direct boost from Earth-zero instead of from a space station, they still needed a few thousand square miles of ocean—and at that you heard ignorant prattle about how the back wash was changing the climate and the government ought to do something.

"Anyhow, there are plenty of brass bands and speeches. We are watching one by the Honorable J. Dillberry Egghead . . . shall I read it back?"

("Uh, don't bother. Who's 'we'?")

"All of us. Faith and Frank just came in."

I was about to ask about Maudie when a new voice came over the system: "Welcome aboard, friends. This is the Captain. We will break loose at an easy three gravities; nevertheless, I want to warn you to relax and keep your arms inside your couches. The triple boost will last only six minutes, then you will be allowed to get up. We take off in number-two position, just after the *Henry Hudson*."

I repeated to Pat what the Captain was saying practically as fast as he said it; this was one of the things we had practiced while he was at the training center: letting your directed thoughts echo what somebody else was saying so that a telepair acted almost like a microphone and a speaker. I suppose he was doing the same at the other end, echoing the Captain's words to the family a split second behind me—it's not hard with practice.

The Captain said, "The *Henry* is on her final run-down . . . ten seconds . . . five seconds . . . *now!*"

I saw something like heat lightning even though I was in a closed room. For a few seconds there was a sound over the speaker like sleet on a window, soft and sibilant and far away. Pat said, *"Boy!"*

("What is it, Pat?")

"She got up out of there as if she had sat on a bee. Just a hole in the water and a flash of light. Wait a sec—they're shifting the view pick-up from the space station to Luna."

("You've got a lot better view than I have. All I can see is the ceiling of this room.")

The female voice said, "Mr. Warner! Miss Furtney! Tweenships telepairs start recording."

The Captain said, "All hands, ready for boost. Stand by for count down," and another voice started in, "Sixty seconds . . . fifty-five . . . fifty . . . forty-five . . . holding on forty-five . . . holding forty-five . . . holding . . . holding . . ." —until I was ready to scream.

"Tom, what's wrong?"

("How should I know?")

"Forty . . . thirty-five . . . thirty . . ."

"Tom, Mum wants me to tell you to be very careful."

("What does she think I can do? I'm just lying here, strapped down.")

"I know." Pat chuckled. *"Hang on tight to the brush,*

you lucky stiff; they are about to take away the ladder."

". . . four! . . . three! . . . two! . . . ONE!"

I didn't see a flash, I didn't hear anything. I simply got very heavy—like being on the bottom of a football pile-up.

"There's nothing but steam where you were."

I didn't answer, I was having trouble breathing.

"They've shifted the pick-up. They're following you with a telephoto now. Tom, you ought to see this . . . you look just like a sun. It burns the rest of the picture right out of the tank."

("How can I see it?") I said crossly. ("I'm *in* it.")

"You sound choked up. Are you all right?"

("You'd sound choked, too, if you had sand bags piled across your chest.")

"Is it bad?"

("It's not good. But it's all right, I guess.")

Pat let up on me and did a right good job of describing what he was seeing by television. The *Richard E. Byrd* took off just after we did, before we had finished the high boost to get escape velocity from Earth; he told me all about it. I didn't have anything to say anyhow; I couldn't see anything and I didn't feel like chattering. I just wanted to hold still and feel miserable.

I suppose it was only six minutes but it felt more like an hour. After a long, long time, when I had decided the controls were jammed and we were going to keep on at high boost until we passed the speed of light, the pressure suddenly relaxed and I felt light as a snowflake . . . if it hadn't been for the straps I would have floated up to the ceiling.

"We have reduced to one hundred and ten per cent of one gravity," the Captain said cheerfully. "Our cruising boost will be higher, but we will give the newcomers among us a while to get used to it." His tone changed and he said briskly, "All stations, secure from blast-off and set space watches, third section."

I loosened my straps and sat up and then stood up. Maybe we were ten per cent heavy, but it did not feel like it; I felt fine. I started for the door, intending to look around more than I had been able to when I came aboard.

Dusty Rhodes yelled at me. "Hey! Come back here and unstrap me! That moron fastened the buckles out of my reach."

I turned and looked at him. "Say 'please.'"

What Dusty answered was not "please." Nevertheless I let him loose. I should have made him say it; it might have saved trouble later.

VII 19,900 WAYS

The first thing that happened in the *L.C.* made me think I was dreaming—I ran into Uncle Steve.

I was walking along the circular passageway that joined the staterooms on my deck and looking for the passage inboard, toward the axis of the ship. As I turned the corner I bumped into someone. I said, "Excuse me," and started to go past when the other person grabbed my arm and clapped me on the shoulder. I looked up and it was Uncle Steve, grinning and shouting at me. "Hi, shipmate! Welcome aboard!"

"Uncle Steve! What are *you* doing here?"

"Special assignment from the General Staff . . . to keep *you* out of trouble."

"Huh?"

There was no mystery when he explained. Uncle Steve had known for a month that his application for special discharge to take service with the LRF for Project Lebensraum had been approved; he had not told the family but had spent the time working a swap to permit him to be in the same ship as Pat—or, as it turned out, the one I was in.

"I thought your mother might take it easier if she knew I was keeping an eye on her boy. You can tell her about it the next time you are hooked in with your twin."

"I'll tell her now," I answered and gave a yell in my mind for Pat. He did not seem terribly interested; I guess a reaction was setting in and he was sore at me for being where he had expected to be. But Mother was there and he said he would tell her. "Okay, she knows."

Uncle Steve looked at me oddly. "Is it as easy as that?"

I explained that it was just like talking . . . a little faster, maybe, since you can think words faster than you can talk, once you are used to it. But he stopped me. "Never mind. You're trying to explain color to a blind man. I just wanted Sis to know."

"Well, okay." Then I noticed that his uniform was different. The ribbons were the same and it was an LRF company uniform, like my own, which did not surprise me—but his chevrons were gone. "Uncle Steve . . . you're wearing major's leaves!"

He nodded. "Home town boy makes good. Hard work, clean living, and so on."

"Gee, that's swell!"

"They transferred me at my reserve rank, son, plus one bump for exceptionally neat test papers. Fact is, if I had stayed with the Corps, I would have retired as a ship's sergeant at best—there's no promotion in peacetime. But the Project was looking for certain men, not certain ranks, and I happened to have the right number of hands and feet for the job."

"Just what is your job, Uncle?"

"Commander of the ship's guard."

"Huh? What have you got to guard?"

"That's a good question. Ask me in a year or two and I can give you a better answer. Actually, 'Commander Landing Force' would be a better title. When we locate a likely looking planet—'when and if,' I mean—I'm the laddie who gets to go out and check the lay of the land and whether the natives are friendly while you valuable types stay safe and snug in the ship." He glanced at his wrist. "Let's go to chow."

I wasn't hungry and wanted to look around, but Uncle Steve took me firmly by the arm and headed for the mess room. "When you have soldiered as long as I have, lad, you will learn that you sleep when you get a chance and that you are never late for chow line."

It actually was a chow line, cafeteria style. The *L.C.* did not run to table waiters nor to personal service of any sort, except for the Captain and people on watch. We went through the line and I found that I was hungry after all. That meal only, Uncle Steve took me over to the heads-of-departments table. "Ladies and gentlemen, this is my nephew with two heads, Tom Bartlett. He left his other head dirtside —he's a telepair twin. If he does anything he shouldn't, don't tell me, just clobber him." He glanced at me; I was turning red. "Say 'howdy,' son . . . or just nod if you can't talk."

I nodded and sat down. A sweet old girl with the sort of lap babies like to sit on was next to me. She smiled and said, "Glad to have you with us, Tom." I learned that she was the Chief Ecologist. Her name was Dr. O'Toole, only nobody called her that, and she was married to one of the relativists.

Uncle Steve went around the table, pointing out who was who and what they did: the Chief Engineer, the Relativist (Uncle Steve called him the "Astrogator" as the job would be called in an ordinary ship), Chief Planetologist Harry Gates and the Staff Xenologist, and so forth—I couldn't remember the names at the time—and Reserve Captain Urqhardt. I didn't catch the word "reserve" and was surprised at how young he was. But Uncle Steve corrected me: "No, no! He's not *the* Captain. He's the man who will be captain if it turns out we need a spare. Across from you is the Surgeon—don't let that fool you, either; he never does surgery himself. Dr. Devereaux is the boss head-shrinker."

I looked puzzled and Uncle Steve went on, "You don't savvy? Psychiatrist. Doc Dev is watching every move we make, trying to decide how quick he will have to be with the straitjacket and the needle. Correct, Doc?"

Dr. Devereaux buttered a roll. "Essentially, Major. But

finish your meal; we're not coming for you until later in the day." He was a fat little toad, ugly as could be, and with a placid, unbreakable calm. He went on, "I just had an up-setting thought, Major."

"I thought that thoughts never upset you?"

"Consider. Here I am charged with keeping quaint charac-ters like you sane . . . but they forgot to assign anybody to keep *me* sane. What should I do?"

"Mmm . . ." Uncle Steve seemed to study it. "I didn't know that head-shrinkers were supposed to be sane, themselves."

Dr. Devereaux nodded. "You've put your finger on it. As in your profession, Major, being crazy is an asset. Pass the salt, please."

Uncle Steve shut up and pretended to wipe off blood.

A man came in and sat down; Uncle Steve introduced me and said, "Staff Commander Frick, the Communications Officer. Your boss, Tom."

Commander Frick nodded and said, "Aren't you third section, young man?"

"Uh, I don't know, sir."

"I do . . . and you should have known. Report to the communications office."

"Uh, you mean now, sir?"

"Right away. You are a half hour late."

I said, "Excuse me," and got up in a hurry, feeling silly. I glanced at Uncle Steve but he wasn't looking my way; he seemed not to have heard it.

The communications office was two decks up, right under the control room; I had trouble finding it. Van Houten was there and Mei-Ling and a man whose name was Travers, who was communicator-of-the-watch. Mei-Ling was reading a sheaf of papers and did not look up; I knew that she was telepathing. Van said, "Where the deuce have you been? I'm hungry."

"I didn't know," I protested.

"You're supposed to know."

He left and I turned to Mr. Travers. "What do you want me to do?"

He was threading a roll of tape into an autotransmitter; he

finished before he answered me. "Take that stack of traffic as she finishes it, and do whatever it is you do with it. Not that it matters."

"You mean read it to my twin?"

"That's what I said."

"Do you want him to record?"

"Traffic is always recorded. Didn't they teach you anything?"

I thought about explaining that they really hadn't because there had not been time, when I thought, oh what's the use? He probably thought I was Pat and assumed that I had had the full course. I picked up papers Mei-Ling was through with and sat down.

But Travers went on talking. "I don't know what you freaks are up here for now anyhow. You're not needed; we're still in radio range."

I put the papers down and stood up. "Don't call us 'freaks.' "

He glanced at me and said, "My, how tall you've grown. Sit down and get to work."

We were about the same height but he was ten years older and maybe thirty pounds heavier. I might have passed it by if we had been alone, but not with Mei-Ling present. "I said not to call us 'freaks.' It's not polite."

He looked tired and not amused but he didn't stand up. I decided he didn't want a fight and felt relieved. "All right, all right," he answered. "Don't be so touchy. Get busy on that traffic."

I sat down and looked over the stuff I had to send, then called Pat and told him to start his recorder; this was not a practice message.

He answered, *"Call back in half an hour. I'm eating dinner."*

("I was eating lunch but I didn't get to finish. Quit stalling, Pat. Take a look at that contract you were so anxious to sign.")

"You were just as anxious. What's the matter, kid? Cold feet already?"

("Maybe, maybe not. I've got a hunch that this isn't go

ing to be one long happy picnic. But I've learned one thing already; when the Captain sends for a bucket of paint, he wants a full bucket and no excuses. So switch on that recorder and stand by to take down figures.")

Pat muttered and gave in, then announced that he was ready after a delay that was almost certainly caused by Mother insisting that he finish dinner. *"Ready."*

The traffic was almost entirely figures (concerning the take-off, I suppose) and code. Being such, I had to have Pat repeat back everything. It was not hard, but it was tedious. The only message in clear was one from the Captain, ordering roses sent to a Mrs. Detweiler in Brisbane and charged to his LRF account, with a message: "Thanks for a wonderful farewell dinner."

Nobody else sent personal messages; I guess they had left no loose ends back on Earth.

I thought about sending some roses to Maudie, but I didn't want to do it through Pat. It occurred to me that I could do it through Mei-Ling, then I remembered that, while I had money in the bank, I had appointed Pat my attorney; if I ordered them, he would have to okay the bill.

I decided not to cross any bridges I had burned behind me.

Life aboard the *L.C.*, or the *Elsie* as we called her, settled into a routine. The boost built up another fifteen per cent which made me weigh a hundred and fifty-eight pounds; my legs ached until I got used to it—but I soon did; there are advantages in being kind of skinny. We freaks stood a watch in five, two at a time—Miss Gamma and Cas Warner were not on our list because they hooked sidewise with other ships. At first we had a lot of spare time, but the Captain put a stop to that.

Knowing that the LRF did not really expect us to return, I had not thought much about that clause in the contract which provided for tutoring during the trip but I found out that the Captain did not intend to forget it. There was school for everybody, not just for us telepaths who were still of school age. He appointed Dr. Devereaux, Mrs. O'Toole, and

Mr. Krishnamurti a school board and courses were offered in practically everything, from life drawing to ancient history. The Captain himself taught that last one; it turned out he knew Sargon the Second and Socrates like brothers.

Uncle Alfred tried to sign up for everything, which was impossible, even if he didn't eat, sleep, nor stand watch. He had never, he told me, had time for all the schooling he wanted and now at last he was going to get it. Even my real uncle, Steve, signed up for a couple of courses. I guess I showed surprise at this, for he said, "Look, Tom, I found out my first cruise that the only way to make space bearable is to have something to learn and learn it. I used to take correspondence courses. But this bucket has the finest assemblage of really bright minds you are ever likely to see. If you don't take advantage of it, you are an idiot. Mama O'Toole's cooking course, for example: where else can you find a *Cordon Bleu* graduate willing to teach you her high art free? I ask you!"

I objected that I would never need to know how to cook high cuisine.

"What's that got to do with it? Learning isn't a means to an end; it is an end in itself. Look at Uncle Alf. He's as happy as a boy with a new slingshot. Anyhow, if you don't sign up for a stiff course, old Doc Devereaux will find some way to keep you busy, even if it is counting rivets. Why do you think the Captain made him chairman of the board of education?"

"I hadn't thought about it."

"Well, think about it. The greatest menace in space is going coffin crazy. You are shut up for a long time in a small space and there is nothing outside but some mighty thin vacuum . . . no street lights, no bowling alleys. Inside are the same old faces and you start hating them. So a smart captain makes sure you have something to keep you interested and tired—and ours is the smartest you'll find or he wouldn't be on this trip."

I began to realize that a lot of arrangements in the *Elsie* were simply to see that we stayed healthy and reasonably happy. Not just school, but other things. Take the number we had aboard, for example—almost two hundred. Uncle Steve told me that the *Elsie* could function as a ship with about ten: a captain, three control officers, three engineer officers, one communicator, one farmer, and a cook. Shucks, you could cut that to five: two control officers (one in command), two torch watchstanders, and a farmer-cook.

Then why two hundred?

In the first place there was room enough. The *Elsie* and the other ships had been rebuilt from the enormous freighters the LRF use to haul supplies out to Pluto and core material back to Earth. In the second place they needed a big scientific staff to investigate the planets we hoped to find. In the third place some were spare parts, like Reserve Captain Urqhardt and, well, me myself. Some of us would die or get killed; the ship had to go on.

But the real point, as I found out, is that no small, isolated social group can be stable. They even have a mathematics for it, with empirical formulas and symbols for "lateral pressures" and "exchange valences" and "exogamic relief." (That last simply means that the young men of a small village should find wives outside the village.)

Or look at it this way. Suppose you had a one-man space ship which could cruise alone for several years. Only a man who was already nutty a certain way could run it—otherwise he would soon go squirrelly some other way and start tearing the controls off the panels. Make it a two-man ship: even if you used a couple as fond of each other as Romeo and Juliet, by the end of the trip even Juliet would start showing black-widow blood.

Three is as bad or worse, particularly if they gang up two against one. Big numbers are much safer. Even with only two hundred people there are exactly nineteen thousand nine hundred ways to pair them off, either as friends or enemies, so you see that the social possibilities shoot up rapidly when you increase the numbers. A bigger group means more chances to find friends and more ways to avoid people you don't like. This is terribly important aboard ship.

Besides elective courses we had required ones called "ship's training"—by which the Captain meant that everybody had to learn at least one job he had not signed up for. I stood two watches down in the damping room, whereupon Chief Engineer Roch stated in writing that he did not think that I would ever make a torcher as I seemed to have an innate lack of talent for nuclear physics. As a matter of fact it made me nervous to be that close to an atomic power plant and to realize the unleashed hell that was going on a few feet away from me.

I did not make out much better as a farmer, either. I spent two weeks in the air-conditioning plant and the only thing I did right was to feed the chickens. When they caught me cross-pollinating the wrong way some squash plants which were special pets of Mrs. O'Toole, she let me go, more in sorrow than in anger. "Tom," she said, "what do you do well?"

I thought about it. "Uh, I can wash bottles . . . and I used to raise hamsters."

So she sent me over to the research department and I washed beakers in the chem lab and fed the experimental animals. The beakers were unbreakable. They wouldn't let me touch the electron microscope. It wasn't bad—I could have been assigned to the laundry.

Out of the 19,900 combinations possible in the *Elsie*, Dusty Rhodes and I were one of the wrong ones. I hadn't signed up for the life sketching class because he was teaching it; the little wart really was a fine draftsman. I know, I'm pretty good at it myself and I would have liked to have been in that class. What was worse, he had an offensively high I.Q., genius plus, much higher than mine, and he could argue rings around me. Along with that he had the manners of a pig and the social graces of a skunk—a bad go, any way you looked at it.

"Please" and "Thank you" weren't in his vocabulary. He never made his bed unless someone in authority stood over him, and I was likely as not to come in and find him lying on mine, wrinkling it and getting the cover dirty. He never hung up his clothes, he always left our wash basin filthy, and his best mood was complete silence.

Besides that, he didn't bathe often enough. Aboard ship that is a crime.

First I was nice to him, then I bawled him out, then I threatened him. Finally I told him that the next thing of his I found on my bed was going straight into the mass converter. He just sneered and the next day I found his camera on my bed and his dirty socks on my pillow.

I tossed the socks into the wash basin, which he had left filled with dirty water, and locked his camera in my wardrobe, intending to let him stew before I gave it back.

He didn't squawk. Presently I found his camera gone from my wardrobe, in spite of the fact that it was locked with a combination which Messrs. Yale & Towne had light-heartedly described as "Invulnerable." My clean shirts were gone, too . . . that is, they weren't clean; somebody had carefully dirtied every one of them.

I had not complained about him. It had become a point of pride to work it out myself; the idea that I could not cope with somebody half my size and years my junior did not appeal to me.

But I looked at the mess he had made of my clothes and and I said to myself, "Thomas Paine, you had better admit that you are licked and holler for help—else your only chance will be to plead justifiable homicide."

But I did not have to complain. The Captain sent for me; Dusty had complained about me instead.

"Bartlett, young Rhodes tells me you are picking on him. What's the situation from your point of view?"

I started to swell up and explode. Then I let out my breath and tried to calm down; the Captain really wanted to know.

"I don't think so, sir, though it is true that we have not been getting along."

"Have you laid hands on him?"

"Uh . . . I haven't smacked him, sir. I've jerked him off my bed more than once—and I wasn't gentle about it."

He sighed. "Maybe you should have smacked him. Out of my sight, of course. Well, tell me about it. Try to tell it straight—and complete."

So I told him. It sounded trivial and I began to be ashamed of myself . . . the Captain had more important things to worry about than whether or not I had to scrub out a hand basin before I could wash my face. But he listened.

Instead of commenting, maybe telling me that I should be able to handle a younger kid better, the Captain changed the subject.

"Bartlett, you saw that illustration Dusty had in the ship's paper this morning?"

"Yes, sir. A real beauty," I admitted. It was a picture of the big earthquake in Santiago, which had happened after we left Earth.

"Mmm . . . we have to allow you special-talent people a little leeway. Young Dusty is along because he was the only m-r available who could receive and transmit pictures."

"Uh, is that important, sir?"

"It could be. We won't know until we need it. But it could be crucially important. Otherwise I would never have permitted a spoiled brat to come aboard this ship." He frowned. "However, Dr. Devereaux is of the opinion that Dusty is not a pathological case."

"Uh, I never said he was, sir."

"Listen, please. He says that the boy has an unbalanced personality—a brain that would do credit to a grown man but with greatly retarded social development. His attitudes and evaluations would suit a boy of five, combined with this clever brain. Furthermore Dr. Devereaux says that he will force the childish part of Dusty's personality to grow up, or he'll turn in his sheepskin."

"So? I mean, 'Yes, sir?' "

"So you should have smacked him. The only thing wrong with that boy is that his parents should have walloped him, instead of telling him how bright he was." He sighed again. "Now I've got to do it. Dr. Devereaux tells me I'm the appropriate father image."

"Yes, sir."

" 'Yes, sir,' my aching head. This isn't a ship; it's a confounded nursery. Are you having any other troubles?"

"No, sir."

"I wondered. Dusty also complained that the regular communicators call you people 'freaks.' " He eyed me.

I didn't answer. I felt sheepish about it.

"In any case, they won't again. I once saw a crewman try to knife another one, just because the other persisted in calling him 'skin head.' My people are going to behave like ladies and gentlemen or I'll bang some heads together." He frowned. "I'm moving Dusty into the room across from my cabin. If Dusty will leave you alone, you let him alone. If he won't . . . well, use your judgment, bearing in mind that you are responsible for your actions—but remember that I don't expect any man to be a doormat. That's all. Goodby."

VIII   RELATIVITY

I had been in the *Elsie* a week when it was decided to operate on Pat. Pat told me they were going to do it, but he did not talk about it much. His attitude was the old iron-man, as if he meant to eat peanuts and read comics while they were chopping on him. I think he was scared stiff . . . I would have been.

Not that I would have understood if I had known the details; I'm no neural surgeon, nor any sort; removing a splinter is about my speed.

But it meant we would be off the watch list for a while, so I told Commander Frick. He already knew from messages passed between the ship and LRF; he told me to drop off the watch list the day before my brother was operated and to consider myself available for extra duty during his convalescence. It did not make any difference to him; not only were there other telepairs but we were still radio-linked to Earth.

Two weeks after we started spacing and the day before Pat was to be cut on I was sitting in my room, wondering whether to go to the communications office and offer my valuable services in cleaning waste baskets and microfilming files or just sit tight until somebody sent for me.

I had decided on the latter, remembering Uncle Steve's advice never to volunteer, and was letting down my bunk, when the squawker boomed: "T. P. Bartlett, special communicator, report to the Relativist!"

I hooked my bunk up while wondering if there was an Eye-Spy concealed in my room—taking down my bunk during working hours seemed always to result in my being paged. Dr. Babcock was not in the control room and they chased me out, but not before I took a quick look around—the control room was off limits to anyone who did not work there. I found him down in the computation room across from the communications office, where I would have looked in the first place if I hadn't wanted to see the control room.

I said, "T. P. Bartlett, communicator tenth grade, reporting to the Relativist as ordered."

Dr. Babcock swung around in his chair and looked at me. He was a big raw-boned man, all hands and feet, and looked more like a lumberjack than a mathematical physicist. I think he played it up—you know, elbows on the table and bad grammar on purpose. Uncle Steve said Babcock had more honorary degrees than most people had socks.

He stared at me and laughed. "Where did you get that fake military manner, son? Siddown. You're Bartlett?"

I sat. "Yes, sir."

"What's this about you and your twin going off the duty list?"

"Well, my brother is in a hospital, sir. They're going to do something to his spine tomorrow."

"Why didn't you tell me?" I didn't answer because it was so unreasonable; I wasn't even in his department. "Frick never tells me anything, the Captain never tells me anything, now you never tell me anything. I have to hang around the galley and pick up gossip to find out what's going on. I was planning on working you over tomorrow. You know that, don't you?"

"Uh, no, sir."

"Of course you don't, because I never tell anybody anything either. What a way to run a ship! I should have stayed in Vienna. There's a nice town. Ever have coffee and pastries in the Ring?" He didn't wait for an answer. "Nevertheless I was going to work you and your twin over tomorrow—so now we'll have to do it today. Tell him to stand by."

"Uh, what do you want him to do, Doctor? He's already been moved to a hospital."

"Just tell him to stand by. I'm going to calibrate you two, that's what. Figure out your index error."

"Sir?"

"Just tell him."

So I called Pat. I hadn't spoken to him since breakfast; I wondered how he was going to take it.

But he already knew. *"Yes, yes,"* he said in a tired voice. *"They're setting up apparatus in my hospital room right now. Mother made such a fuss I had to send her out."*

("Look, Pat, if you don't want to do this, whatever it is, I'll tell them nothing doing. It's an imposition.")

"What difference does it make?" he said irritably. *"I've got to sweat out the next sixteen hours somehow. Anyhow, this may be the last time we work together."*

It was the first time he had shown that it was affecting his nerve. I said hastily, ("Don't talk that way, Pat. You're going to get well. You're going to walk again. Shucks, you'll even be able to ski if you want to.")

"Don't give me that Cheerful Charlie stuff. I'm getting more of it from the folks than I can use. It makes me want to throw up."

("Now see here, Pat—")

"Stow it, stow it! Let's get on with what they want us to do."

("Well, all right.") I spoke aloud: "He's ready, Doctor."

77

"Half a minute. Start your camera, O'Toole." Dr. Babcock touched something on his desk. "Commander Frick?"

"Yes, Doctor," Frick's voice answered.

"We're ready. You coming in?"

"All set here," I heard my boss answer. "We'll come in."

A moment later he entered, with Anna Horoshen. In the meantime I took a look around. One whole wall of the computation room was a computer, smaller than the one at Los Alamos but not much. The blinking lights must have meant something to somebody. Sitting at right angles to it at a console was Mr. O'Toole and above the console was a big display scope; at about one-second intervals a flash of light would peak in the center of it.

Anna nodded without speaking; I knew she must be linked. Pat said, *"Tom, you've got a girl named Anna Horoshen aboard. Is she around?"*

("Yes. Why?")

"Say hello to her for me—I knew her in Zurich. Her sister Becky is here." He chuckled and I felt better. *"Good looking babes, aren't they? Maudie is jealous."*

Babcock said to Frick, "Tell them to stand by. First synchronizing run, starting from their end."

"Tell them, Anna."

She nodded. I wondered why they bothered with a second telepair when they could talk through myself and Pat. I soon found out: Pat and I were too busy.

Pat was sounding out ticks like a clock; I was told to repeat them . . . and every time I did another peak of light flashed on the display scope. Babcock watched it, then turned me around so that I couldn't see and taped a microphone to my voice box. "Again."

Pat said, *"Stand by—"* and started ticking again. I did my best to tick right with him but it was the silliest performance possible. I heard Babcock say quietly, "That cut out the feedback and the speed-of-sound lag. I wish there were some way to measure the synaptic rate more closely."

Frick said, "Have you talked to Dev about it?"

I went on ticking.

"A reverse run now, young lady," Babcock said, and

slipped headphones on me. I immediately heard a ticking like the ticks Pat had been sending. "That's a spectral metronome you're listening to, young fellow, timed by monochrome light. It was synchronized with the one your brother is using before we left Earth. Now start ticking at him."

So I did. It had a hypnotic quality; it was easier to get into step and tick with it than it was to get out of step. It was impossible to ignore it. I began to get sleepy but I kept on ticking; I couldn't stop.

"End of run," Babcock announced. The ticking stopped and I rubbed my ears.

"Dr. Babcock?"

"Huh?"

"How can you tell one tick from another?"

"Eh? *You* can't. But O'Toole can, he's got it all down on film. Same at the other end. Don't worry about it; just try to stay in time."

This silliness continued for more than an hour, sometimes with Pat sending, sometimes myself. At last O'Toole looked up and said, "Fatigue factor is cooking our goose, Doc. The second differences are running all over the lot."

"Okay, that's all," Babcock announced. He turned to me. "You can thank your brother for me and sign off."

Commander Frick and Anna left. I hung around. Presently Dr. Babcock looked up from his desk and said, "You can go, bub. Thanks."

"Uh, Dr. Babcock?"

"Huh? Speak up."

"Would you mind telling me what this is all about?"

He looked surprised, then said, "Sorry. I'm not used to using people instead of instruments; I forget. Okay, sit down. This is why you m-r people were brought along: for research into the nature of time."

I stared. "Sir? I thought we were along to report back on the planets we expect to find."

"Oh, that— Well, I suppose so, but this is much more important. There are too many people as it is; why encourage new colonies? A mathematician could solve the population problem in jig time—just shoot every other one."

Mr. O'Toole said, without looking up, "The thing I like about you, Chief, is your big warm heart."

"Quiet in the gallery, please. Now today, son, we have been trying to find out what time it is."

I must have looked as puzzled as I felt for he went on, "Oh, we *know* what time it is . . . but too many different ways. See that?" He pointed at the display scope, still tirelessly making a peak every second. "That's the Greenwich time tick, pulled in by radio and corrected for relative speed and change of speed. Then there is the time you were hearing over the earphones; that is the time the ship runs by. Then there is the time you were getting from your brother and passing to us. We're trying to compare them all, but the trouble is that we have to have people in the circuit and, while a tenth of a second is a short time for the human nervous system, a microsecond is a measurably long time in physics. Any radar system splits up a microsecond as easily as you slice a pound of butter. So we use a lot of runs to try to even out our ignorance."

"Yes, but what do you expect to find out?"

"If I 'expected,' I wouldn't be doing it. But you might say that we are trying to find out what the word 'simultaneous' means."

Mr. O'Toole looked up from the console. "If it means anything," he amended.

Dr. Babcock glanced at him. "You still here? 'If it means anything.' Son, ever since the great Doctor Einstein, 'simultaneous' and 'simultaneity' have been dirty words to physicists. We chucked the very concept, denied that it had meaning, and built up a glorious structure of theoretical physics without it. Then you mind readers came along and kicked it over. Oh, don't look guilty; every house needs a housecleaning now and then. If you folks had done your carnival stunt at just the speed of light, we would have assigned you a place in the files and forgotten you. But you rudely insisted on doing it at something enormously greater than the speed of light, which made you as welcome as a pig at a wedding. You've split us physicists into two schools,

80

those who want to class you as a purely psychological phe-
nomenon and no business of physics—these are the 'close
your eyes and it will go away' boys—and a second school
which realizes that since measurements can be made of whatever this is you do, it is therefore the business of physics
to measure and include it . . . since physics is, above all,
the trade of measuring things and assigning definite nu-
merical values to them."

O'Toole said, "Don't wax philosophical, Chief."

"You get back to your numbers, O'Toole; you have no
soul. These laddies want to measure how fast you do it. They
don't care how fast—they've already recovered from the
blow that you do it faster than light—but they want to
know exactly how fast. They can't accept the idea that you
do it 'instantaneously,' for that would require them to go
to a different church entirely. They want to assign a definite
speed of propagation, such-and-such number of times faster
than the speed of light. Then they can modify their old
equations and go right on happily doing business at the
old stand."

"They will," agreed O'Toole.

"Then there is a third school of thought, the right one . . .
my own."

O'Toole, without looking up, made a rude noise.

"Is that your asthma coming back?" Babcock said anxiously. "By the way, you got any results?"

"They're still doing it in nothing flat. Measured time negative as often as positive and never greater than inherent ob-
servational error."

"You see, son? That's the correct school. Measure what
happens and let the chips fly where they may."

"Hear, hear!"

"Quiet, you renegade Irishman. Besides that, you m-r's
give us our first real chance to check another matter. Are
you familiar with the relativity transformations?"

"You mean the Einstein equations?"

"Surely. You know the one for time?"

I thought hard. Pat and I had taken first-year physics

our freshman year; it had been quite a while. I picked up a piece of paper and wrote down what I thought it was:

$$t_1 = t\sqrt{1 - \frac{v^2}{c^2}}$$

"That's it," agreed Dr. Babcock. "At a relative velocity of 'v' time interval at first frame of reference equals time interval at second frame of reference multiplied by the square root of one minus the square of the relative velocity divided by the square of the speed of light. That's just the special case, of course, for constant speeds; it is more complicated for acceleration. But there has been much disagreement as to what the time equations meant, or if they meant anything."

I blurted out, "Huh? But I thought the Einstein theory had been proved?" It suddenly occurred to me that, if the relativity equations were wrong, we were going to be away a mighty long time—Tau Ceti, our first stop, was eleven light-years from the Sun . . . and that was just our first one; the others were a lot farther.

But *everybody* said that once we got up near the speed of light the months would breeze past like days. The equations *said* so.

"Attend me. How do you prove that there are eggs in a bird's nest? Don't strain your gray matter: go climb the tree and find out. There is no other way. Now we are climbing the tree."

"Fine!" said O'Toole. "Go climb a tree."

"Noisy in here. One school of thought maintained that the equations simply meant that a clock would read differently if you could read it from a passing star . . . which you can't . . . but that there was no real stretching or shrinking of time—whatever 'real' means. Another school pointed to the companion equations for length and mass, maintaining that the famous Michelson-Morley experiment showed that the length transformation was 'real' and pointing out that the increase of mass was regularly computed and used for particle-accelerator ballistics and elsewhere in nuclear physics

—for example, in the torch that pushes this ship. So, they reasoned, the change in time rates must be real, because the corollary equations worked in practice. But nobody knew. You have to climb the tree and look."

"When will we know?" I was still worrying. Staying several years, Einstein time, in the ship I had counted on. Getting killed in the course of it, the way Uncle Steve said we probably would, I refused to worry about. But dying of old age in the *Elsie* was not what I had counted on. It was a grim thought, a life sentence shut up inside these steel walls.

"When? Why, we know right now."

"You do? What's the answer?"

"Don't hurry me, son. We've been gone a couple of weeks, at a boost of 124% of one gee; we're up to about 9,000 miles per second now. We still haven't come far—call it seven and a half light-hours or about 5,450,000,000 miles. It will be the better part of a year before we are crowding the speed of light. Nevertheless we have reached a sizable percentage of that speed, about five per cent; that's enough to show. Easy to measure, with the aid of you mind readers."

"Well, sir? Is it a real time difference? Or is it just relative?"

"You're using the wrong words. But it's 'real,' so far as the word means anything. The ratio right now is about 99.9%."

"To put it exactly," added Mr. O'Toole, "Bartlett's slippage—that's a technical term I just invented—his 'slippage' in time rate from that of his twin has now reached twelve parts in ten thousand."

"So you would make me a liar for one fiftieth of one per cent?" Babcock complained. "O'Toole, why did I let you come along?"

"So you would have some one to work your arithmetic," his assistant answered smugly.

Pat told me he did not want me around when they operated, but I came anyway. I locked myself in my room so nobody could disturb me and stuck with him. He didn't really object; whenever I spoke he answered and the closer it got to the deadline the more he talked . . . a cheerful babble about nothing and everything. It did not fool me.

When they wheeled him into surgery, he said, "Tom, you should see my anesthetist. Pretty as a sunny day and just lap size."

("Isn't her face covered with a mask?")

"Well, not completely. I can see her pretty blue eyes. I think I'll ask her what she's doing tonight."

("Maudie won't like that.")

"You keep Maudie out of this; a sick man is entitled to privileges. Wait a sec, I'll ask her."

("What did she say?")

"She said, 'Nothing much,' and that I would be doing the same for a few days. But I'll get her phone number."

("Two gets you five she won't give it to you.")

"Well, I can try . . . uh uh! Too late, they're starting in . . . Tom, you wouldn't believe this needle; it's the size of an air hose. She says she wants me to count. Okay, anything for a laugh . . . one . . . two . . . three . . ."

Pat got up to seven and I counted with him. All the way through I kept winding up tighter and tighter to unbearable tension and fear. I knew now what he apparently had been sure of all along, that he was not coming out of it. At the count of seven he lost track but his mind did not go silent. Maybe those around the operating table thought they had him unconscious but I knew better; he was trapped inside and screaming to get out.

I called to him and he called back but we couldn't find each other. Then I was as trapped and lost and confused as he was and we groped around in the dark and the cold and the aloneness of the place where you die.

Then I felt the knife whittling at my back and I screamed.

The next thing I remember is a couple of faces floating over me. Somebody said, "I think he's coming around, Doctor." The voice did not belong to anyone; it was a long way off.

Then there was just one face and it said, "Feeling better?"

"I guess so. What happened?"

"Drink this. Here, I'll hold up your head."

When I woke up again I felt fairly wide awake and could see that I was in the ship's infirmary. Dr. Devereaux was there, looking at me. "You decided to come out of it, young fellow?"

"Out of what, Doctor? What happened?"

"I don't know precisely, but you gave a perfect clinical picture of a patient terminating in surgical shock. By the time we broke the lock on your door, you were far gone—you gave us a bad time. Can you tell me about it?"

I tried to think, then I remembered. Pat! I called him in my mind. ("*Pat!* Where are you, boy?")

He didn't answer. I tried again and he still didn't answer, so I knew. I sat up and managed to choke out, "My brother . . . he *died!*"

Dr. Devereaux said, "Wups! Take it easy. Lie down. He's not dead . . . unless he died in the last ten minutes, which I doubt."

"But I can't reach him! How do you know? I can't reach him, I tell you!"

"Come down off the ceiling. Because I've been checking on him all morning via the m-r's on watch. He's resting easily under an eighth grain of hypnal, which is why you can't raise him. I may be stupid, son—I *was* stupid, not to warn you to stay out of it—but I've been tinkering with the human mind long enough to figure out approximately what happened to you, given the circumstances. My only excuse is that I have never encountered such circumstances before."

I quieted a little. It made sense that I couldn't wake Pat if they had him under drugs. Under Dr. Devereaux's questions I managed to tell him more or less what had happened —not perfectly, because you can't really tell someone else what goes on inside your head. "Uh, was the operation successful, Doctor?"

"The patient came through in good shape. We'll talk about it later. Now turn over."

"Huh?"

"Turn over. I want to take a look at your back."

He looked at it, then called two of his staff to see it. Presently he touched me. "Does that hurt?"

"Ouch! Uh, yes, it's pretty tender. What's wrong with my back, Doctor?"

"Nothing, really. But you've got two perfect stigmata, just matching the incisions for Macdougal's operation . . . which is the technique they used on your brother."

"Uh, what does that mean?"

"It means that the human mind is complicated and we don't know much about it. Now roll over and go to sleep. I'm going to keep you in bed a couple of days."

I didn't intend to go to sleep but I did. I was awakened by Pat calling me. *"Hey, Tom! Where are you? Snap out of it."*

("I'm right here. What's the matter?")

"Tom . . . I've got my legs back!"

I answered, ("Yeah, I know,") and went back to sleep.

IX RELATIVES

Once Pat was over his paralysis I should have had the world by the tail, for I had everything I wanted. Somehow it did not work that way. Before he was hurt, I had known why I was down in the dumps: it was because he was going and I wasn't. After he was hurt, I felt guilty because I was getting what I wanted through his misfortune. It didn't seem right to be happy when he was crippled—especially when his crippled condition had got me what I wanted.

So I should have been happy once he was well again.

Were you ever at a party where you were supposed to be having fun and suddenly you realized that you weren't? No reason, just no fun and the whole world gray and taste-less?

Some of the things that were putting me off my feed I could see. First there had been Dusty, but that had been cleared up. Then there had been the matter of other people, especially the electron pushers we stood watch with, calling us freaks and other names and acting as if we were. But the Captain had tromped on that, too, and when we got better acquainted people forgot about such things. One of the rela-tivists, Janet Meers, was a lightning calculator, which made her a freak, too, but everybody took it for granted in her and after a while they took what we did for granted.

After we got out of radio range of Earth the Captain took us out from under Commander Frick and set us up as a department of our own, with "Uncle" Alfred McNeil as head of department and Rupert Hauptman as his assistant—which meant that Rupe kept the watch list while Uncle Alf was in charge of our mess table and sort of kept us in line. We liked old Unc too well to give him much trouble and if somebody did get out of line Unc would look sad and the rest of us would slap the culprit down. It worked.

I think Dr. Devereaux recommended it to the Captain. The fact was that Commander Frick resented us. He was an electrical engineer and had spent his whole life on better and better communication equipment . . . then we came along and did it better and faster with no equipment at all. I don't blame him; I would have been sore, too. But we got along better with Uncle Alf.

I suppose that the *Vasco da Gama* was part of my trouble. The worst thing about space travel is that absolutely nothing happens. Consequently the biggest event in our day was the morning paper. All day long each mind reader on watch (when not busy with traffic, which wasn't much) would copy news. We got the news services free and all the features and Dusty would dress it up by copying pictures sent by his twin Rusty. The communicator on the midwatch would edit it and the m-r and the communicator on the early morning watch would print it and have it in the mess room by breakfast.

There was no limit to the amount of copy we could have; it was just a question of how much so few people could prepare. Besides Solar System news we carried ships' news, not only of the *Elsie* but of the eleven others. Everybody (except myself) knew people in the other ships. Either they had met them at Zurich, or the old spacehands, like the Captain and a lot of others, had friends and acquaintances reaching back for years.

It was mostly social news, but we enjoyed it more than news from Earth and the System, because we felt closer to the ships in the fleet, even though they were billions of miles away and getting farther by the second. When Ray Gilberti and Sumire Watanabe got married in the *Leif Ericsson*, every ship in the fleet held a celebration. When a baby was born in the *Pinta* and our Captain was named godfather, it made us all proud.

We were hooked to the *Vasco da Gama* through Cas Warner, and Miss Gamma Furtney linked us with the *Marco Polo* and the *Santa Maria* through her triplets Miss Alpha and Miss Beta, but we got news from all the ships by pass-down-the-line. Fleet news was never cut, even if dirtside news had to be. As it was, Mama O'Toole complained that if the editions got any larger, she would either have to issue clean sheets and pillow cases only once a week or engineering would have to build her another laundry just to wash newspapers. Nevertheless, the ecology department always had clean paper ready, freshly pressed, for each edition.

We even put out an occasional extra, like the time Lucille LaVonne won "Miss Solar System" and Dusty did a pic of her so perfect you would have sworn it was a photograph. We lost some paper from that as quite a number of people kept their copies for pin-ups instead of turning them back for reclamation—I did myself. I even got Dusty to autograph it. It startled him but pleased him even though he was rude about it—an artist is entitled to credit for his work, I say, even if he is a poisonous little squirt.

What I am trying to say is that the *Elsie Times* was the

high point of each day and fleet news was the most important part of it.

I had not been on watch the night before; nevertheless, I was late for breakfast. When I hurried in, everybody was busy with his copy of the *Times* as usual—but nobody was eating. I sat down between Van and Prudence and said, "What's the matter? What's aching everybody?"

Pru silently handed me a copy of the *Times*.

The first page was bordered in black. There were oversize headlines: *VASCO DA GAMA LOST*

I couldn't believe it. The *Vasco* was headed out for Alpha Centauri but she wouldn't get there for another four years, Earth time; she wasn't even close to the speed of light. There was nothing to have any trouble with, out where she was. It must be a mistake.

I turned to see-story-on-page-two. There was a boxed dispatch from the Commodore in the *Santa Maria*: "(Official) At 0334 today Greenwich time TS *Vasco da Gama* (LRF 172) fell out of contact. Two special circuits were operating at the time, one Earthside and one to the *Magellan*. In both cases transmission ceased without warning, in midst of message and at the same apparent instant by adjusted times. The ship contained eleven special communicators; it has not proved possible to raise any of them. It must therefore be assumed that the ship is lost, with no survivors."

The LRF dispatch merely admitted that the ship was out of contact. There was a statement by our Captain and a longer news story which included comments from other ships; I read them but the whole story was in the headlines . . . the *Vasco* was gone wherever it is that ships go when they don't come back.

I suddenly realized something and looked up. Cas Warner's chair was empty. Uncle Alf caught my eye and said quietly, "He knows, Tom. The Captain woke him and told him soon after it happened. The only good thing about it is that he wasn't linked with his brother when it happened."

I wasn't sure that Uncle Alf had the right slant. If Pat got it, I'd want to be with him when it happened, wouldn't I? Well, I thought I would. In any case I was sure that Unc would want to be holding Sugar Pie's hand if something happened and she had to make the big jump before he did. And Cas and his brother Caleb were close; I knew that.

Later that day the Captain held memorial services and Uncle Alfred preached a short sermon and we all sang the "Prayer for Travelers." After that we pretended that there never had been a ship named the *Vasco da Gama*, but it was all pretense.

Cas moved from our table and Mama O'Toole put him to work as an assistant to her. Cas and his brother had been hotel men before LRF tapped them and Cas could be a lot of help to her; keeping a ship with two hundred people in it in ecological balance is no small job. Goodness, just raising food for two hundred people would be a big job even if it did not have to be managed so as to maintain atmospheric balance; just managing the yeast cultures and the hydroponics took all the time of nine people.

After a few weeks Cas was supervising catering and housekeeping and Mama O'Toole could give all of her time to the scientific and technical end—except that she continued to keep an eye on the cooking.

But the *Vasco da Gama* should not have made me brood; I didn't know anybody in that ship. If Cas could pull out of it and lead a normal, useful life, I certainly should not have had the mulligrubs. No, I think it was my birthday as much as anything.

The mess room had two big electric clocks in it, controlled from the relativists' computation room, and two bank-style calendars over them. When we started out they were all right together, showing Greenwich time and date. Then, as we continued to accelerate and our speed got closer to that of light, the "slippage" between *Elsie* and the Earth began to show and they got farther and farther out of phase. At first we talked about it, but presently we didn't notice the Greenwich set . . . for what good does it do you to know that it is now three in the morning next Wednesday at Greenwich when it is lunch time in the ship? It was like time zones and the date line back on Earth: not ordinarily important. I didn't even notice when Pat groused about the odd times of day he had to be on duty because I stood watches any time of day myself.

Consequently I was caught flat-footed when Pat woke me with a whistle in the middle of the night and shouted, *"Happy birthday!"*

("Huh? Whose?")

"Yours, dopey. Ours. What's the matter with you? Can't you count?"

("But—")

"Hold it. They are just bringing the cake in and they are going to sing 'Happy Birthday.' I'll echo it for you."

While they were doing so I got up and slipped on a pair of pants and went down to the mess room. It was the middle of "night" for us and there was just a standing light here. But I could see the clocks and calendars—sure enough, the Greenwich date was our birthday and figuring back zone time from Greenwich to home made it about dinner time at home.

But it *wasn't* my birthday. I was on the other schedule and it didn't seem right.

"Blew 'em all out, kid," Pat announced happily. *"That ought to hold us for another year. Mum wants to know if they baked a cake for you there?"*

("Tell her 'yes.' ") They hadn't, of course. But I didn't feel like explaining. Mother got jittery easily enough without trying to explain Einstein time to her. As for Pat, he ought to know better.

The folks had given Pat a new watch and he told me that there was a box of chocolates addressed to me—should he open it and pass it around? I told him to go ahead, not knowing whether to be grateful that I was remembered or to be annoyed at a "present" I couldn't possibly see or touch. After a while I told Pat that I had to get my sleep and please say good night and thank you to everybody for me. But I didn't get to sleep; I lay awake until the passageway lights came on.

The following week they did have a birthday cake for me at our table and everybody sang to me and I got a lot of pleasantly intended but useless presents—you can't give

91

a person much aboard ship when you are eating at the same mess and drawing from the same storerooms. I stood up and thanked them when somebody hollered "Speech!" and I stayed and danced with the girls afterwards. Nevertheless it still did not seem like my birthday because it had already *been* my birthday, days earlier.

It was maybe the next day that my Uncle Steve came around and dug me out of my room. "Where you been keeping yourself, youngster?"

"Huh? Nowhere."

"That's what I thought." He settled in my chair and I lay back down on my bunk. "Every time I look for you, you aren't in sight. You aren't on watch or working all the time. Where are you?"

I didn't say anything. I had been right where I was a lot of the time, just staring at the ceiling. Uncle Steve went on, "When a man takes to crouching in a corner aboard ship, it is usually best, I've found, to let him be. Either he will pull out of it by himself, or he'll go out the airlock one day without bothering with a pressure suit. Either way, he doesn't want to be monkeyed with. But you're my sister's boy and I've got a responsibility toward you. What's wrong? You never show up for fun and games in the evenings and you go around with a long face; what's eating you?"

"There's nothing wrong with me!" I said angrily.

Uncle Steve disposed of that with a monosyllable. "Open up, kid. You haven't been right since the *Vasco* was lost. Is that the trouble? Is your nerve slipping? If it is, Doc Devereaux has synthetic courage in pills. Nobody need know you take 'em and no need to be ashamed—everybody finds a crack in his nerve now and again. I'd hate to tell you what a repulsive form it took the first time I went into action."

"No, I don't think that is it." I thought about it—maybe it was it. "Uncle Steve, what happened to the *Vasco?*"

He shrugged. "Either her torch cut loose, or they bumped into something."

"But a torch *can't* cut loose . . . can it? And there is nothing to bump into out here."

"Correct on both counts. But suppose the torch did blow?"

The ship would be a pocket-sized *nova* in an umpteenth second. But I can't think of an easier way to go. And the other way would be about as fast, near enough you would never notice. Did you ever think how much kinetic energy we have wrapped up in this bucket at this speed? Doc Babcock says that as we reach the speed of light we'll be just a flat wave front, even though we go happily along eating mashed potatoes and gravy and never knowing the difference."

"But we never quite reach the speed of light."

"Doc pointed that out, too. I should have said 'if.' Is that what is bothering you, kid? Fretting that we might go *boom!* like the *Vasco?* If so, let me point out that almost all the ways of dying in bed are worse . . . particularly if you are silly enough to die of old age—a fate I hope to avoid."

We talked a while longer but did not get anywhere. Then he left, after threatening to dig me out if I spent more than normal sack time in my room. I suppose Uncle Steve reported me to Dr. Devereaux, although both of them claimed not.

Anyhow, Dr. Devereaux tackled me the next day, took me around to his room and sat me down and talked to me. He had a big sloppy-comfortable stateroom; he never saw anybody in surgery.

I immediately wanted to know why he wanted to talk to me.

He opened his frog eyes wide and looked innocent. "Just happened to get around to you, Tom." He picked up a pile of punched cards. "See these? That's how many people I've had a chat with this week. I've got to pretend to earn my pay."

"Well, you don't have to waste time on me. I'm doing all right."

"But I like to waste time, Tom. Psychology is a wonderful racket. You don't scrub for surgery, you don't have to stare down people's dirty throats, you just sit and pretend to listen while somebody explains that when he was a little boy he didn't like to play with the other little boys. Now you talk for a while. Tell me anything you want to, while I take a nap. If you talk long enough, I can get rested up from the poker party I sat in on last night and still chalk up a day's work."

I tried to talk and say nothing. While I was doing so, Pat called me. I told him to call back; I was busy. Dr. Devereaux was watching my face and said suddenly, "What was on your mind then?"

I explained that it could wait; my twin wanted to talk to me.

"Hmm . . . Tom, tell me about your twin. I didn't have time to get well acquainted with him in Zurich."

Before I knew it I had told him a lot about both of us. He was remarkably easy to talk to. Twice I thought he had gone to sleep but each time I stopped, he roused himself and asked another question that got me started all over again.

Finally he said, "You know, Tom, identical twins are exceptionally interesting to psychologists—not to mention geneticists, sociologists, and biochemists. You start out from the same egg, as near alike as two organic complexes can be. Then you become two different people. Are the differences environmental? Or is there something else at work?"

I thought about this. "You mean the soul, Doctor?"

"Mmm . . . ask me next Wednesday. One sometimes holds personal and private views somewhat different from one's public and scientific opinions. Never mind. The point is that you m-r twins are interesting. I fancy that the serendipitous results of Project Lebensraum will, as usual, be far greater than the intended results."

"The 'Sarah' what, Doctor?"

"Eh? 'Serendipitous.' The Adjective for 'Serendipity.' Serendipity means that you dig for worms and strike gold. Happens all the time in science. It is the reason why 'useless' pure research is always so much more practical than 'practical' work. But let's talk about you. I can't help you with your problems—you have to do that yourself. But let's kick it around and pretend that I can, so as to justify my being on the payroll. Now two things stick out like a sore thumb: the first is that you don't like your brother."

I started to protest but he brushed it aside. "Let me talk.

Why are you sure that I am wrong? Answer: because you have been told from birth that you love him. Siblings always 'love' each other; that is a foundation of our civilization, like Mom's apple pie. People usually believe anything that they are told early and often. Probably a good thing they believe this one, because brothers and sisters often have more opportunity and more reason to hate each other than anyone else."

"But I *like* Pat. It's just—"

" 'It's just' what?" he insisted gently when I did not finish.

I did not answer and he went on, "It is just that you have every reason to dislike him. He has bossed you and bullied you and grabbed what he wanted. When he could not get it by a straight fight, he used your mother to work on your father to make it come his way. He even got the girl you wanted. Why should you like him? If a man were no relation—instead of being your twin brother—would you like him for doing those things to you? Or would you hate him?"

I didn't relish the taste of it. "I wasn't being fair to him, Doctor. I don't think Pat knew he was hogging things . . . and I'm sure our parents never meant to play favorites. Maybe I'm just feeling sorry for myself."

"Maybe you are. Maybe there isn't a word of truth in it and you are constitutionally unable to see what's fair when you yourself are involved. But the point is that this is the way you do feel about it . . . and you certainly would not like such a person—except that he is your twin brother, so of course you must 'love' him. The two ideas fight each other. So you will continue to be stirred up inside until you figure out which one is false and get rid of it. That's up to you."

"But . . . doggone it, Doctor, I *do* like Pat!"

"Do you? Then you had better dig out of your mind the notion that he has been handing you the dirty end of the stick all these years. But I doubt if you do. You're fond of him—we're all fond of things we are used to, old shoes, old pipes, even the devil we know is better than a strange devil. You're loyal to him. He's necessary to you and you are necessary to him. But 'like' him? It seems most improbable. On the other hand, if you could get it through your head that there is no longer any need to 'love' him, nor even to like him, then you might possibly get to like him a little for what he is. You'll certainly grow more tolerant of him, though I doubt if you will ever like him much. He's a rather unlikeable cuss."

"That's not true! Pat's always been very popular."

"Not with me. Mmm . . . Tom, I cheated. I know your brother better than I let on. Neither one of you is very likeable, matter of fact, and you are very much alike. Don't take offense. I can't abide 'nice' people; 'sweetness and light' turns my stomach. I like ornery people with a good, hard core of self-interest—a lucky thing, in view of my profession. You and your brother are about equally selfish, only he is more successful at it. By the way, he likes you."

"Huh?"

"Yes. The way he would a dog that always came when called. He feels protective toward you, when it doesn't conflict with his own interests. But he's rather contemptuous of you; he considers you a weakling—and, in his book, the meek are not entitled to inherit the earth; that's for chaps like himself."

I chewed that over and began to get angry. I did not doubt that Pat felt that way about me—patronizing and willing to see to it that I got a piece of cake . . . provided that he got a bigger one.

"The other thing that stands out," Dr. Devereaux went on, "is that neither you nor your brother wanted to go on this trip."

This was so manifestly untrue and unfair that I opened my mouth and left it open. Dr. Devereaux looked at me. "Yes? You were about to say?"

"Why, that's the silliest thing I ever heard, Doctor! The only real trouble Pat and I ever had was because both of us wanted to go and only one of us could."

He shook his head. "You've got it backwards. Both of you wanted to stay behind and only one of you could. Your brother won, as usual."

"No, he didn't . . . well, yes, he did, but the chance to go;

96

not the other way around. And he would have, too, if it hadn't been for that accident."

" 'That accident.' Mmm . . . yes." Dr. Devereaux held still, with his head dropped forward and his hands folded across his belly, for so long that I thought again that he was asleep. "Tom, I'm going to tell you something that is none of your business, because I think you need to know. I suggest that you never discuss it with your twin . . . and if you do, I'll make you out a liar, net. Because it would be bad for him. Understand me?"

"Then don't tell me," I said surlily.

"Shut up and listen." He picked up a file folder. "Here is a report on your brother's operation, written in the talk we doctors use to confuse patients. You wouldn't understand it and, anyhow, it was sent sidewise, through the *Santa Maria* and in code. You want to know what they found when they opened your brother up?"

"Uh, not especially."

"There was no damage to his spinal cord of any sort."

"Huh? Are you trying to tell me that he was *faking* his legs being paralyzed? I don't believe it!"

"Easy, now. He wasn't faking. His legs *were* paralyzed. He could not possibly fake paralysis so well that a neurologist could not detect it. I examined him myself; your brother was paralyzed. But not from damage to his spinal cord—which I knew and the surgeons who operated on him knew."

"But—" I shook my head. "I guess I'm stupid."

"Aren't we all? Tom, the human mind is not simple; it is very complex. Up at the top, the conscious mind has its own ideas and desires, some of them real, some of them impressed on it by propaganda and training and the necessity for putting up a good front and cutting a fine figure to other people. Down below is the unconscious mind, blind and deaf and stupid and sly, and with—usually—a different set of desires and very different motivations. It wants its own way . . . and when it doesn't get it, it raises a stink until it is satisfied. The trick in easy living is to find out what your unconscious mind really wants and give it to it on the cheapest terms possible, before it sends you through emotional bankruptcy to get its own way. You know what a psychotic is, Tom?"

"Uh . . . a crazy person."

" 'Crazy' is a word we're trying to get rid of. A psychotic is a poor wretch who has had to sell out the shop and go naked to the world to satisfy the demands of his unconscious mind. He's made a settlement, but it has ruined him. My job is to help people make settlements that won't ruin them—like a good lawyer. We never try to get them to evade the settlement, just arrange it on the best terms.

"What I'm getting at is this: your brother managed to make a settlement with his unconscious on fairly good terms, very good terms considering that he did it without professional help. His conscious mind signed a contract and his unconscious said flatly that he must not carry it out. The conflict was so deep that it would have destroyed some people. But not your brother. His unconscious mind elected to have an accident instead, one that could cause paralysis and sure enough it did—*real* paralysis, mind you; no fakery. So your brother was honorably excused from an obligation he could not carry out. Then, when it was no longer possible to go on this trip, he was operated on. The surgery merely corrected minor damage to the bones. But he was encouraged to think that his paralysis would go away—and so it did." Devereaux shrugged.

I thought about it until I was confused. This conscious and unconscious stuff—I'd studied it and passed quizzes in it . . . but I didn't take any stock in it. Doc Devereaux could talk figures of speech until he was blue in the face but it didn't get around the fact that both Pat and I had wanted to go and the only reason Pat had to stay behind was because he had hurt himself in that accident. Maybe the paralysis was hysterical, maybe he had scared himself into thinking he was hurt worse than he was. But that didn't make any difference.

But Doc Devereaux talked as if the accident wasn't an accident. Well, what of it? Maybe Pat was scared green and had been too proud to show it—I still didn't think he had taken a tumble on a mountainside on purpose.

In any case, Doc was dead wrong on one thing: *I* had wanted to go. Oh, maybe I had been a little scared and I knew I had been homesick at first—but that was only natural.

("Then why are you so down in dumps, stupid?")

That wasn't Pat talking; that was me, talking to myself. Shucks, maybe it was my unconscious mind, talking out loud for once.

"Doc?"

"Yes, Tom."

"You say I didn't really want to come along?"

"It looks that way."

"But you said the unconscious mind always wins. You can't have it both ways."

He sighed. "That isn't quite what I said. You were hurried into this. The unconscious is stupid and often slow; yours did not have time to work up anything as easy as a skiing accident. But it is stubborn. It's demanding that you go home . . . which you can't. But it won't listen to reason. It just keeps on nagging you to give it the impossible, like a baby crying for the moon."

I shrugged. "To hear you tell it, I'm in an impossible mess."

"Don't look so danged sourpuss! Mental hygiene is a process of correcting the correctable and adjusting to the inevitable. You've got three choices."

"I didn't know I had any."

"Three. You can keep on going into a spin until your mind builds up a fantasy acceptable to your unconscious . . . a psychotic adjustment, what you would call 'crazy.' Or you can muddle along as you are, unhappy and not much use to yourself or your shipmates . . . and always with the possibility of skidding over the line. Or you can dig into your own mind, get acquainted with it, find out what it really wants, show it what it can't have and why, and strike a healthy bargain with it on the basis of what is possible. If you've got guts and gumption, you'll try the last one. It won't be easy." He waited, looking at me.

"Uh, I guess I'd better try. But how do I do it?"

"Not by moping in your room about might-have-beens, that's sure."

"My Uncle Steve—Major Lucas, I mean"—I said slowly, "told me I shouldn't do that. He wants me to stir around and associate with other people. I guess I should."

"Surely, surely. But that's not enough. You can't chin yourself out of the hole you are in just by pretending to be the life of the party. You have to get acquainted with yourself."

"Yes, sir. But *how?*"

"Well, we can't do it by having you talk about yourself every afternoon while I hold your hand. Mmm . . . I suggest that you try writing down who you are and where you've been and how you got from there to here. You make it thorough enough and maybe you will begin to see 'why' as well as 'how.' Keep digging and you may find out who you are and what you want and how much of it you can get."

I must have looked baffled for he said, "Do you keep a diary?"

"Sometimes. I've got one along."

"Use it as an outline. 'The Life and Times of T. P. Bartlett, Gent.' Make it complete and try to tell the truth—all the truth."

I thought that over. Some things you don't want to tell anybody. "Uh, I suppose you'll want to read it, Doctor?"

"Me? Heaven forbid! I get too little rest without misguided people. This is for *you*, son; you'll be writing to yourself . . . only write it as if you didn't know anything about yourself and had to explain everything. Write it as if you expected to lose your memory and wanted to be sure you could pick up the strings again. Put it all down." He frowned and added grudgingly, "If you feel that you have found out something important and want a second opinion, I suppose I could squeeze in time to read part of it, at least. But I won't promise. Just write it to yourself—to the one with amnesia."

So I told him I would try . . . and I have. I can't see that it has done any special good (I pulled out of the slump anyhow) and there just isn't time to do the kind of job he told me to do. I've had to hurry over the last part of this because this is the first free evening I've had in a month.

But it's amazing how much you can remember when you really try.

X   RELATIONS

There have been a lot of changes around the *Elsie*. For one thing we are over the hump now and backing down the other side, decelerating as fast as we boosted; we'll be at Tau Ceti in about six months, ship's time.

But I am getting ahead of myself. It has been about a year, S-time, since I started this, and about twelve years, Earth time, since we left Earth. But forget E-time; it doesn't mean anything. We've been thirteen months in the ship by S-time and a lot has happened. Pat getting married—no, that didn't happen in the ship and it's the wrong place to start.

Maybe the place to start is with another marriage, when Chet Travers married Mei-Ling Jones. It met with wide approval, except on the part of one of the engineers who was sweet on her himself. It caused us freaks and the electron pushers to bury the hatchet to have one of us marry one of them, especially when Commander Frick came down the aisle in the mess room with the bride on his arm, looking as proud and solemn as if she had been his daughter. They were a good match; Chet was not yet thirty and I figure that Mei-Ling is at least twenty-two.

But it resulted in a change in the watch list and Rupe put me on with Prudence Mathews.

I had always liked Pru without paying much attention to her. You had to look twice to know that she was pretty. But she had a way of looking up at you that made you feel important. Up to the time I started standing watches with her I had more or less left the girls alone; I guess I was "being true to Maudie." But by then I was writing this confession story for Doc Devereaux; somehow writing things down gives them finality. I said to myself, "Why not? Tom, old boy, Maudie is as definitely out of your life as if one of you were dead. But life goes on, right here in this bucket of wind."

I didn't do anything drastic; I just enjoyed Pru's company as much as possible . . . which turned out to be a lot.

I've heard that when the animals came aboard the *Ark* two by two, Noah separated them port and starboard. The *Elsie* isn't run that way. Chet and Mei-Ling had found it possible to get well enough acquainted to want to make it permanent. A little less than half of the crew had come aboard as married couples; the rest of us didn't have any obstacles put in our way if we had such things on our minds.

But somehow without its ever showing we were better chaperoned than is usual back dirtside. It didn't seem organized . . . and yet it must have been. If somebody was saying good night a little too long in a passageway after the lights were dimmed, it would just happen that Uncle Alfred had to get up about then and shuffle down the passageway. Or maybe it would be Mama O'Toole, going to make herself a cup of chocolate "to help her get to sleep."

Or it might be the Captain. I think he had eyes in the back of his head for everything that went on in the ship. I'm convinced that Mama O'Toole had. Or maybe Unc was actually one of those hypothetical wide-range telepaths but was too polite and too shrewd to let anybody know it.

Or maybe Doc Devereaux had us all so well analyzed in those punched cards of his that he always knew which way the rabbit would jump and could send his dogs to head him off. I wouldn't put it past him.

But it was always just enough and not too much. Nobody

objected to a kiss or two if somebody wanted to check on the taste; on the other hand we never had any of the scandals that pop up every now and then in almost any community. I'm sure we didn't; you can't keep such things quiet in a ship. But nobody seemed to see a little low-pressure lalligagging.

Certainly Pru and I never did anything that would arouse criticism.

Nevertheless we were taking up more and more of each other's time, both on and off watch. I wasn't serious, not in the sense of thinking about getting married; but I was serious in that it was becoming important. She began to look at me privately and a bit possessively, or maybe our hands would touch in passing over a stack of traffic and we could feel the sparks jump.

I felt fine and alive and I didn't have time to write in these memoirs. I gained four pounds and I certainly wasn't homesick.

Pru and I got in the habit of stopping off and raiding the pantry whenever we came off a night watch together. Mama O'Toole didn't mind; she left it unlocked so that anyone who wanted a snack could find one—she said this was our home, not a jail. Pru and I would make a sandwich, or concoct a creative mess, and eat and talk before we turned in. It didn't matter what we talked about; what mattered was the warm glow we shared.

We came off watch at midnight one night and the mess room was deserted; the poker players had broken up early and there wasn't even a late chess game. Pru and I went into the pantry and were just getting set to grill a yeast-cheese sandwich. The pantry is rather cramped; when Pru turned to switch on the small grill, she brushed against me.

I got a whiff of her nice, clean hair and something like fresh clover or violets. Then I put my arms around her.

She didn't make any fuss. She stopped dead for an instant, then she relaxed.

Girls are nice. They don't have any bones and I think they must be about five degrees warmer than we are, even if fever thermometers don't show it. I put my face down and she put her face up and closed her eyes and everything was wonderful.

For maybe half a second she kissed me and I knew she was as much in favor of it as I was, which is as emphatic as I can put it.

Then she had broken out of my arms like a wrestler and was standing pressed against the counter across from me and looking terribly upset. Well, so was I. She wasn't looking at me; she was staring at nothing and seemed to be listening ... so I knew; it was the expression she wore when she was linked—only she looked terribly unhappy too.

I said, "Pru! What's the matter?"

She did not answer; she simply started to leave. She had taken a couple of steps toward the door when I reached out and grabbed her wrist. "Hey, are you mad at me?"

She twisted away, then seemed to realize that I was still there. "I'm sorry, Tom," she said huskily. "My sister is angry."

I had never met Patience Mathews—and now I hardly wanted to. "Huh? Well, of all the silly ways to behave I—"

"My sister doesn't like you, Tom," she answered firmly, as if that explained everything. "Good night."

"But—"

"Good night, Tom."

Pru was as nice as ever at breakfast but when she passed me the rolls the sparks didn't jump. I wasn't surprised when Rupe reshuffled the watch list that day but I did not ask why. Pru didn't avoid me and she would even dance with me when there was dancing, but the fire was out and neither of us tried to light it again.

A long time later I told Van about it. I got no sympathy. "Think you're the first one to get your finger mashed in the door? Pru is a sweet little trick, take it from Grandfather van Houten. But when Sir Galahad himself comes riding up on a white charger, he's going to have to check with Patience before he can speak to Pru ... and I'll bet you the answer is 'No!' Pru is willing, in her sweet little half-witted way, but

104

Patience won't okay anything more cozy than 'Pease Porridge Hot.' "

"I think it's a shame. Mind you, it doesn't matter to me now. But her sister is going to ruin her life."

"It's her business. Myself, I reached a compromise with my twin years ago—we beat each other's teeth in and after that we cooperated on a businesslike basis. Anyhow, how do you know that Pru isn't doing the same to Patience? Maybe Pru started it."

It didn't sour me on girls, not even on girls who had twin sisters who were mind readers, but after that I enjoyed the company of all of them. But for a while I saw more of Unc. He liked to play dominoes, then when we had finished all even up for the evening he liked to talk about Sugar Pie—and *to* her, of course. He would look at his big photograph of her and so would I and the three of us would talk, with Unc echoing for both of us. She really was a nice little girl and it was a lot of fun to get to know a little six-year-old girl—it's very quaint what they think about.

One night I was talking with them and looking at her picture, as always, when it occurred to me that time had passed and that Sugar Pie must have changed—they grow up fast at that age. I got a brilliant idea. "Unc, why don't you have Sugar Pie mail a new photograph to Rusty Rhodes? Then he could transmit it to Dusty and Dusty could draw you one as perfect as that one, only it would be up to date, show you what she looks like now, huh? How about it, Sugar Pie? Isn't that a good idea?"

"It isn't necessary."

I was looking at the picture and I nearly popped my fuses. For a moment it wasn't the same picture. Oh, it was the same merry little girl, but she was a little older, she was shy a front tooth, and her hair was different.

"And she was alive. Not just a trukolor stereo, but alive. There's a difference.

But when I blinked it was the same old picture.

I said hoarsely, "Unc, who said, 'It isn't necessary?' You? Or Sugar Pie?"

"Why, Sugar Pie did. I echoed."

"Yes, Unc . . . but I didn't hear *you*; I heard *her*." Then I told him about the photograph.

He nodded. "Yes, that's the way she looks. She says to tell you that her tooth is coming in, however."

"Unc . . . there's no way to get around it. For a moment I crowded in on your private wave length." I was feeling shaky.

"I knew. So did Sugar Pie. But you didn't crowd in, son; a friend is always welcome."

I was still trying to soak it in. The implications were more mind-stretching, even, than when Pat and I found out we could do it. But I didn't know what they were yet. "Uh, Unc, do you suppose we could do it again? Sugar Pie?"

"We can try."

But it didn't work . . . unless I heard her voice as well as Unc's when she said, "Good night, Tommie." I wasn't sure.

After I got to bed I told Pat about it. He was interested after I convinced him that it really had happened. *"This is worth digging into, old son. I'd better record it. Doc Mabel will want to kick it around."*

("Uh, wait until I check with Uncle Alf.")

"Well, all right. I guess it is his baby . . . in more ways than one. Speaking of his baby, maybe I should go see her? With two of us at each end it might be easier to make it click again. Where does his niece live?"

("Uh, Johannesburg.")

"Mmm . . . that's a far stretch down the road, but I'm sure the LRF would send me there if Doc Mabel got interested."

("Probably. But let me talk to Unc.")

But Unc talked to Dr. Devereaux first. They called me in and Doc wanted to try it again at once. He was as near excited as I ever saw him get. I said, "I'm willing, but I doubt if we'll get anywhere; we didn't last night. I think that once was just a fluke."

"Fluke, spook. If it can be done once, it can be done again. We've got to be clever enough to set up the proper conditions." He looked at me. "Any objection to a light dose of hypnosis?"

"Me? Why, no, sir. But I don't hypnotize easily."

"So? According to your record, Dr. Arnault found it not impossible. Just pretend I'm she."

I almost laughed in his face. I look more like Cleopatra than he looks like pretty Dr. Arnault. But I agreed to go along with the gag.

"All either of you will need is a light trance to brush distractions aside and make you receptive."

I don't know what a "light trance" is supposed to feel like. I didn't feel anything and I wasn't asleep.

But I started hearing Sugar Pie again.

I think Dr. Devereaux's interest was purely scientific; any new fact about what makes people tick could rouse him out of his chronic torpor. Uncle Alf suggested that Doc was anxious also to set up a new telepathic circuit, just in case. There was a hint in what Unc said that he realized that he himself would not last forever.

But there was a hint of more than that. Uncle Alf let me know very delicately that, if it should come to it, it was good to know that somebody he trusted would be keeping an eye on his baby. He didn't quite say it, not that baldly, so I didn't have to answer, or I would have choked up. It was just understood—and it was the finest compliment I ever received. I wasn't sure I deserved it so I decided I would just have to manage to deserve it if I ever had to pay off.

I could "talk" to Uncle Alf now, of course, as well as to Sugar Pie. But I didn't, except when all three of us were talking together; telepathy is an imposition when it isn't necessary. I never called Sugar Pie by myself, either, save for a couple of test runs for Doc Devereaux's benefit to establish that I *could* reach her without Unc's help. That took drugs; Unc would wake up from an ordinary sleep if anyone shouted on that "wave length." But otherwise I left her alone; I had no business crowding into a little girl's mind unless she was ready and expecting company.

It was shortly after that that Pat got married.

XI SLIPPAGE

My relations with Pat got steadily better all during that first boost, after Dr. Devereaux took me in hand. I found out, after I admitted that I despised and resented Pat, that I no longer did either one. I cured him of bothering me unnecessarily by bothering him unnecessarily—he could shut off an alarm clock but he couldn't shut off me. Then we worked out a live-and-let-live formula and got along better. Presently I found myself looking forward to whatever time we had set for checking with each other and I realized I liked him, not "again" but "at last," for I had never felt that warm toward him before.

But even while we were getting closer we were falling apart; "slippage" was catching up with us. As anyone can see from the relativity formulas, the relationship is not a straight-line one; it isn't even noticeable at the beginning but it builds up like the dickens at the other end of the scale.

At three-quarters the speed of light he complained that I was drawling, while it seemed to me that he was starting to jabber. At nine-tenths of the speed of light it was close to two for one, but we knew what was wrong now and I talked fast and he talked slow.

At 99% of c, it was seven to one and all we could do to make ourselves understood. Later that day we fell out of touch entirely.

Everybody else was having the same trouble. Sure, telepathy is instantaneous, at least the trillions of miles between us didn't cause any lag, not even like the hesitation you get in telephoning from Earth to Luna, nor did the signal strength drop off. But brains are flesh and blood, and thinking takes time . . . and our time rates were out of gear. I was thinking so slowly (from Pat's viewpoint) that he could not slow down and stay with me; as for him, I knew from time to time that he was trying to reach me but it was just a squeal in the earphones so far as making sense was concerned.

Even Dusty Rhodes couldn't make it. His twin couldn't concentrate on a picture for the long hours necessary to let Dusty "see" it.

It was upsetting, to say the least, to all of us. Hearing voices is all right, but not when you can't tell what they are saying and can't shut them off. Maybe some of the odd cases in psychiatry weren't crazy at all; maybe the poor wretches were tuned in on a bad wave length.

Unc took it the worst at first and I sat with him all one evening while we both tried, together. Then he suddenly regained his serenity; Sugar Pie was thinking about him, that he knew; so being, words weren't really necessary.

Pru was the only one who flourished; she was out from under the thumb of her sister. She got really kissed, probably for the first time in her life. No, not by me; I just happened to be wandering down for a drink at the scuttlebutt, then I backed away quietly and let the drink wait. No point in saying who it was, as it didn't mean anything—I think Pru would have kissed the Captain at that point if he had held still. Poor little Pru!

We resigned ourselves to having to wait until we slid back down closer into phase. We were still hooked ship-to-ship because the ships were accelerating to the same schedule, and there was much debate back and forth about the dilemma, one which apparently nobody had anticipated. In one way it was not important, since we would not have anything to report until we slowed down and started checking the stars we were headed for, but in another way it was: the time the *Elsie* spent at the speed of light (minus a gnat's whisker) was going to seem very short to us—but it was going to be ten solid years and a bit over to those back Earthside. As we learned later, Dr. Devereaux and his opposite numbers in the other ships and back in LRF were wondering how many telepathic pairs they would have still functioning (if any) after a lapse of years. They had reason to worry. It had already been established that identical twins were hardly ever telepairs if they had lived apart for years—that was the other reason why most of those picked were young; most twins are separated by adult life.

But up to then, we hadn't been "separated" in Project Lebensraum. Sure, we were an unthinkable distance apart but each pair had been in daily linkage and in constant practice by being required to stand regular watches, even if there was nothing to send but the news.

But what would a few years of being out of touch do to rapport between telepartners?

This didn't bother me; I didn't know about it. I got a sort of an answer out of Mr. O'Toole which caused me to think that a couple of weeks of ship's time would put us back close enough in phase to make ourselves understood. In the meantime, no watches to stand so it wasn't all bad. I went to bed and tried to ignore the squeals inside my head.

I was awakened by Pat.

"*Tom . . . answer me, Tom. Can you hear me, Tom? Answer me.*"

("Hey, Pat, I'm here!") I was wide awake, out of bed and standing on the floor plates, so excited I could hardly talk.

"*Tom! Oh, Tom! It's good to hear you, boy—it's been two years since I was last able to raise you.*"

("But—") I started to argue, then shut up. It had been less than a week to me. But I would have to look at the Greenwich calendar and a check with the computation office before I could even guess how long it had been for Pat.

"*Let me talk, Tom, I can't keep this up long. They've had me under deep hypnosis and drugs for the past six weeks and it has taken me this long to get in touch with you. They don't dare keep me under much longer.*"

("You mean they've got you hypped right now?")

"*Of course, or I couldn't talk to you at all. Now—*" His

110

voice faded out for a second. "*Sorry. They had to stop to give me another shot and an intravenous feeding. Now listen and record this schedule: Van Houten—*" He reeled off precise Greenwich times and dates, to the second, for each of us, and faded out while I was reading them back. I caught a "*So long*" that went up in pitch, then there was silence.

I pulled on pants before I went to wake the Captain but I did not stop for shoes. Then everybody was up and all the daytime lights were turned on even though it was officially night and Mama O'Toole was making coffee and everybody was talking. The relativists were elbowing each other in the computation room and Janet Meers was working out ship's time for Bernie van Houten's appointment with his twin without bothering to put it through the computer because he was first on the list.

Van failed to link with his brother and everybody got jittery and Janet Meers was in tears because somebody suggested that she had made a mistake in the relative times, working it in her head. But Dr. Babcock himself pushed her solution through the computer and checked her to nine decimals. Then he announced in a chilly tone that he would thank everyone not to criticize his staff thereafter; that was his privilege.

Gloria linked with her sister right after that and everybody felt better. The Captain sent a dispatch to the flagship through Miss Gamma and got an answer back that two other ships were back in contact, the *Nautilus* and the *Cristoforo Colombo*.

There was no more straggling up to relieve the watch and stopping to grab a bite as we passed the pantry. If the re-computed time said your opposite number would be ready to transmit at 3:17:06 and a short tick, ship's time, you were waiting for him from three o'clock on and no nonsense, with the recorder rolling and the mike in front of your lips. It was easy for us in the ship, but each one of us knew that his telepair was having to undergo both hypnosis and drastic drugging to stay with us at all—Dr. Devereaux did not seem happy about it.

Nor was there any time for idle chit-chat, not with your

twin having to chop maybe an hour out of his life for each word. You recorded what he sent, right the first time and no fumbles; then you transmitted what the Captain had initialed. If that left a few moments to talk, all right. Usually it did not ... which was how I got mixed up about Pat's marriage.

You see, the two weeks bracketing our change-over from boost to deceleration, during which time we reached our peak speed, amounted to about ten years Earthside. That's 250 to 1 on the average. But it wasn't all average; at the middle of that period the slippage was much greater. I asked Mr. O'Toole what the maximum was and he just shook his head. There was no way to measure it, he told me, and the probable errors were larger than the infinitesimal values he was working with.

"Let's put it this way," he finished. "I'm glad there is no hay fever in this ship, because one hard sneeze would push us over the edge."

He was joking, for, as Janet Meers pointed out, as our speed approached the speed of light, our mass approached infinity.

But we fell out of phase again for a whole day.

At the end of one of those peak "watches" (they were never more than a couple of minutes long, S-time) Pat told me that he and Maudie were going to get married. Then he was gone before I could congratulate him. I started to tell him that I thought Maudie was a little young and wasn't he rushing things, and missed my chance. He was off our band.

I was not exactly jealous. I examined myself and decided that I was not when I found out that I could not remember what Maudie looked like. Oh, I knew what she looked like —blonde, and a little snub nose with a tendency to get freckles across it in the summertime. But I couldn't call up her face the way I could Pru's face, or Janet's. All I felt was a little left out of things.

I did remember to check on the Greenwich, getting Janet to relate it back to the exact time of my last watch. Then I saw that I had been foolish to criticize. Pat was twenty-three and Maudie was twenty-one, almost twenty-two.

I did manage to say, "Congratulations," on my next linkage but Pat did not have a chance to answer. Instead he answered on the next. "Thanks for the congratulations. We've named her after Mother but I think she is going to look like Maudie."

This flabbergasted me. I had to ask for Janet's help again and found that everything was all right—I mean, when a couple has been married two years a baby girl is hardly a surprise, is it? Except to me.

All in all, I had to make quite a few readjustments those two weeks. At the beginning Pat and I were the same age, except for an inconsequential slippage. At the end of that period (I figure the end as being the time when it was no longer necessary to use extreme measures to let us telepairs talk) my twin was more than eleven years older than I was and had a daughter seven years old.

I stopped thinking about Maudie as a girl, certainly not as one I had been sweet on. I decided that she was probably getting fat and sloppy and very, very domestic—she never could resist that second chocolate eclair. As a matter of fact, Pat and I had grown very far apart, for we had little in common now. The minor gossip of the ship, so important to me, bored him; on the other hand, I couldn't get excited about his flexible construction units and penalty dates. We still telecommunicated satisfactorily but it was like two strangers using a telephone. I was sorry, for I had grown to like him before he slipped away from me.

But I did want to see my niece. Knowing Sugar Pie had taught me that baby girls are more fun than puppies and even cuter than kittens. I remembered the idea I had had about Sugar Pie and braced Dusty on the subject.

He agreed to do it; Dusty can't turn down a chance to show how well he can draw. Besides, he had mellowed, for him; he no longer snarled when you tried to pet him even though it might be years before he would learn to sit up and beg.

Dusty turned out a beautiful picture. All Baby Molly lacked was little wings to make her a cherub. I could see a resemblance to myself—to her father, that is. "Dusty, this is a beautiful picture. Is it a good likeness?"

He bristled. "How should I know? But if there is a micron's difference, or a shade or tone off that you could pick up with a spectrophotometer, from the pic your brother mailed to my brother, I'll eat it! But how do I know how the proud parents had the thing prettied up?"

"Sorry, sorry! It's a swell picture. I wish there were some way I could pay you."

"Don't stay awake nights; I'll think of something. My services come high."

I took down my pic of Lucille LaVonne and put Molly in her place. I didn't throw away the one of Lucille, though.

It was a couple of months later that I found out that Dr. Devereaux had seen entirely different possibilities in my being able to use the "wave length" of Uncle Alf and Sugar Pie from the obvious ones I had seen. I had continued to talk with both of them, though not as often as I had at first. Sugar Pie was a young lady now, almost eighteen, in normal school at Witwatersrand and already started practice teaching. Nobody but Unc and I called her "Sugar Pie" and the idea that I might someday substitute for Unc was forgotten —at the rate we were shifting around pretty soon *she* could bring *me* up.

But Doc Devereaux had not forgotten the matter. However the negotiations had been conducted by him with LRF without consulting me. Apparently Pat had been told to keep it to himself until they were ready to try it, for the first I knew of it was when I told him to stand by to record some routine traffic (we were back on regular watches by then). *"Skip it, old son,"* he said. *"Pass the traffic to the next victim. You and I are going to try something fresh."*

("What?")

"LRF orders, all the way down from the top. Molly has an interim research contract all of her own, just like you and I had."

("Huh? She's not a twin.")

"Let me count her. No, there's just one of her—though she sometimes seems like an entire herd of wild elephants. But she's here, and she wants to say hello to Uncle Tom."

("Oh, fine. Hello, Molly.")

"Hello, Uncle Tom."

I almost jumped out of my skin. I had caught it right off, with no fumbling. ("Hey, who was that? Say that again!")

"Hello, Uncle Tom." She giggled. *"I've got a new hair bow."*

I gulped. ("I'll bet you look mighty cute in it, honey. I wish I could see you. Pat! When did this happen?")

"On and off, for the past ten weeks. It took some tough sessions with Dr. Mabel to make it click. By the way, it took some tougher sessions with, uh, the former Miss Kauric before she would agree to let us try it."

"He means Mummy," Molly told me in a conspirator's whisper. *"She didn't like it. But I do, Uncle Tom. I think it's nice."*

"I've got no privacy from either one of them," Pat complained. *"Look, Tom, this is just a test run and I'm signing off. I've got to get the terror back to her mother."*

"She's going to make me take a nap," Molly agreed in a resigned voice, *"and I'm too old for naps. Good-by, Uncle Tom. I love you."*

("I love you, Molly.")

I turned around and Dr. Devereaux and the Captain were standing behind me, ears flapping. "How did it go?" Dr. Devereaux demanded, eagerly—for him.

I tried to keep my face straight. "Satisfactorily. Perfect reception."

"The kid, too?"

"Why, yes, sir. Did you expect something else?"

He let out a long breath. "Son, if you weren't needed, I'd beat your brains out with an old phone list."

I think Baby Molly and I were the first secondary communication team in the fleet. We were not the last. The LRF, proceeding on a hypothesis suggested by the case of Uncle Alfred and Sugar Pie, assumed that it was possible to form a new team where the potential new member was very young and intimately associated with an adult member of an old team. It worked in some cases. In other cases it could not even be tried because no child was available.

Pat and Maude had a second baby girl just before we reached the Tau Ceti system. Maudie put her foot down with respect to Lynette; she said two freaks in her family were enough.

XII TAU CETI

By the time we were a few light-hours from Tau Ceti we knew that we had not drawn a blank; by stereo and doppler-stereo Harry Gates had photographed half a dozen planets. Harry was not only senior planetologist; he was boss of the research department. I suppose he had enough degrees to string like beads, but I called him "Harry" because everybody did. He was not the sort you call "Doctor"; he was eager and seemed younger than he was.

To Harry the universe was a complicated toy somebody had given him; he wanted to take it apart and see what made it go. He was delighted with it and willing to discuss it with anybody at any time. I got acquainted with him in the bottle-washing business because Harry didn't treat lab assistants like robots; he treated them like people and did not mind that he knew so much more than they did—he even seemed to think that he could learn something from them.

How he found time to marry Barbara Kuiper I don't know but Barbara was a torch watchstander, so it probably started as a discussion of physics and drifted over into biology and sociology; Harry was interested in everything. But he didn't find time to be around the night their first baby was born, and that was the night he photographed the planet he named

Constance, after the baby. There was objection to this, because everybody wanted to name it, but the Captain decided that the ancient rule applied: finders of astronomical objects were entitled to name them.

Finding Constance was not an accident. (I mean the planet, not the baby; the baby wasn't lost.) Harry wanted a planet about fifty to fifty-one million miles from Tau, or perhaps I should say that the LRF wanted one of that distance. You see, while Tau Ceti is a close relative of the Sun, by spectral types, Tau is smaller and gives off only about three-tenths as much sunshine—so, by the same old tired inverse square law you use to plan the lights for a living room or to arrange a photoflash picture, a planet fifty million miles from Tau would catch the same amount of sunlight as a planet ninety-three million miles from Sol, which is where Earth sits. We weren't looking for just any planet, or we would have stayed home in the Solar System; we wanted a reasonable facsimile of Earth or it would not be worth colonizing.

If you go up on your roof on a clear night, the stars look so plentiful you would think that planets very much like Earth must be as common as eggs in a hen yard. Well, they are: Harry estimates that there are between a hundred thousand and a hundred million of them in our own Milky Way—and you can multiply that figure by anything you like for the whole universe.

The hitch is that they aren't conveniently at hand. Tau Ceti was only eleven light-years from Earth; most stars in our own Galaxy average more like fifty thousand light-years from Earth. Even the Long Range Foundation did not think in those terms; unless a star was within a hundred light-years or so it was silly to think of colonizing it even with torchships. Sure, a torchship can go as far as necessary, even across the Galaxy—but who is going to be interested in receiving its real estate reports after a couple of ice ages have come and gone? The population problem would be solved one way or another long before then . . . maybe the way the Kilkenny cats solved theirs.

But there are only fifteen-hundred-odd stars within a

hundred light-years of Earth and only about a hundred and sixty of these are of the same general spectral type as the Sun. Project Lebensraum hoped to check not more than half of these, say seventy-five at the outside—less since we had lost the *Vasco da Gama*.

If even *one* real Earth-type planet was turned up in the search, the project would pay off. But there was no certainty that it would. A Sol-type star might not have an Earth-type planet; a planet might be too close to the fire, or too far, or too small to hold an atmosphere, or too heavy for humanity's fallen arches, or just too short on the H_2O that figures into everything we do.

Or it might be populated by some rough characters with notions about finders-keepers.

The *Vasco da Gama* had had the best chance to find the first Earth-type planet as the star she had been heading for, Alpha Centauri Able, is the *only* star in this part of the world which really is a twin of the Sun. (Able's companion, Alpha Centauri Baker, is a different sort, spectral type K.) We had the next best chance, even though Tau Ceti is less like the Sun than is Alpha Centauri-B, for the next closest G-type is about thirteen light years from Earth . . . which gave us a two-year edge over the *Magellan* and nearly four over the *Nautilus*.

Provided we found anything, that is. You can imagine how jubilant we were when Tau Ceti turned out to have pay dirt.

Harry was jubilant, too, but for the wrong reasons. I had wandered into the observatory, hoping to get a sight of the sky—one of the *Elsie*'s shortcomings was that it was almost impossible to see out—when he grabbed me and said, "Look at this, pal!"

I looked at it. It was a sheet of paper with figures on it; it could have been Mama O'Toole's crop-rotation schedule. "What is it?"

"Can't you read? It's Bode's Law, that's what it is!"

I thought back. Let me see . . . no, that was Ohm's Law —then I remembered; Bode's Law was a simple geometrical progression that described the distances of the Solar planets from the Sun. Nobody had ever been able to find a reason for it and it didn't work well in some cases, though I seemed to remember that Neptune, or maybe Pluto, had been discovered by calculations that made use of it. It looked like an accidental relationship.

"What of it?" I asked.

" 'What of it?' the man says! Good grief! This is the most important thing since Newton got conked with the apple."

"Maybe so, Harry, but I'm a little slow today. I thought Bode's Law was just an accident. Why couldn't it be an accident here, too?"

"Accident! Look, Tom, if you roll a seven once, that's an accident. When you roll a seven eight hundred times in a row, somebody has loaded the dice."

"But this is only twice."

"It's not the same thing. Get me a big enough sheet of paper and I'll write down the number of zeros it takes to describe how unlikely this 'accident' is." He looked thoughtful. "Tommie, old friend, this is going to be the key that unlocks how planets are made. They'll bury us right alongside Galileo for this. Mmm . . . Tom, we can't afford to spend much time in this neighborhood; we've got to get out and take a look at the Beta Hydri system and make sure it checks the same way—just to convince the mossbacks back Earthside, for it will, it will! I gotta go tell the Captain we'll have to change the schedule." He stuffed the paper in a pocket and hurried away. I looked around but the anti-radiation shutters were over the observatory ports; I didn't get to see out.

Naturally the Captain did not change the schedule; we were out there looking for farm land, not trying to unscrew the inscrutable. A few weeks later we were in orbit around Constance. It put us into free-fall for the first time during the trip, for we had not even been so during acceleration-deceleration change-over but had done it in a skew path instead; chief engineers don't like to shut a torch down unless there is time for an overhaul before starting up again—there was the case of the *Peter the Great* who shut hers off, couldn't light up again, and fell into the Sun.

I didn't like free-fall. But it's all right if you don't overload your stomach.

Harry did not seem disappointed. He had a whole new planet to play with, so he tabled Bode's Law and got busy. We stayed in orbit, a thousand miles up, while research found out everything possible about Connie without actually touching it: direct visual search, radiation survey, absorption-spectra of her atmosphere. She had two moons, one a nice size, though smaller than Luna, so they were able to measure her surface gravity exactly.

She certainly looked like a home from home. Commander Frick had his boys and girls set up a relay tank in the mess room, with color and exaggerated stero, so that we all could see. Connie looked like the pictures they show of Earth from space stations, green and blue and brown and half covered with clouds and wearing polar ice like skullcaps. Her air pressure was lower than ours but her oxygen ratio was higher; we could breathe it. Absorption spectra showed higher carbon dioxide but not as high as Earth had during the Coal Age.

She was smaller but had a little more land area than Earth; her oceans were smaller. Every dispatch back to Earth carried good news and I even managed to get Pat's mind off his profit-and-loss for a while . . . he had incorporated us as "Bartlett Brothers, Inc." and seemed to expect me to be interested in the bookkeeping simply because my accumulated LRF salary had gone into the capitalization. Shucks, I hadn't touched money for so long I had forgotten anybody used the stuff.

Naturally our first effort was to find out if anybody was already in occupation . . . intelligent animal life I mean, capable of using tools, building things, and organizing. If there was, we were under orders to scoot out of there without landing, find fuel somewhere else in that system, and let a later party attempt to set up friendly relations; the LRF did not want to repeat the horrible mistake that had been made with Mars.

But the electro-magnetic spectrum showed nothing at all, from gamma radiation right up to the longest radio wave

120

lengths. If there were people down there, they didn't use radio and they didn't show city lights and they didn't have atomic power. Nor did they have aircraft, nor roads, nor traffic on the surface of their oceans, nor anything that looked like cities. So we moved down just outside the atmosphere in an "orange slice" pole-to-pole orbit that let us patrol the whole surface, a new sector each half turn.

Then we searched visually, by photography, and by radar. We didn't miss anything more conspicuous than a beaver dam, I'm sure. No cities, no houses, no roads, no bridges, no ships, nobody home. Oh, animals, surely—we could see herds grazing on the plains and we got lesser glimpses of other things. But it looked like a squatter's paradise.

The Captain sent a dispatch: "I am preparing to land."

I promptly volunteered for the reconnaissance party. First I braced my uncle Major Lucas to let me join his guard. He told me to go roll my hoop. "If you think I have any use for an untrained recruit, you're crazier than you apparently think I am. If you wanted to soldier, you should have thought of it as soon as we torched off."

"But you've got men from all the departments in your guard."

"Every one of 'em trained soldiers. Seriously, Tom, I can't afford it. I need men who will protect *me;* not somebody so green I'll have to protect him. Sorry."

So I tackled Harry Gates to let me join the scientific party the ship's guard would protect. He said, "Certainly, why not? Plenty of dirty work that my gang of prima donnas won't want to do. You can start by checking this inventory."

So I checked while he counted. Presently he said, "How does it feel to be a little green man in a flying saucer?"

"What?"

"An oofoe. We're an oofoe, do you realize that?"

I finally understood him—an U.F.O., an "unidentified flying object." There were accounts of the U.F.O. hysteria in all the histories of space flight. "I suppose we *are* an U.F.O., sort of."

"It's exactly what we are. The U.F.O.'s were survey ships, just as we are. They looked us over, didn't like what they saw, and went away. If they hadn't found Earth crawling with hostile natives, they would have landed and set up housekeeping, just as we are going to do."

"Harry, do you *really* believe the U.F.O.'s were anything but imagination or mistakes in reporting? I thought that theory was exploded long ago."

"Take another look at the evidence, Tom. There was *something* going on up in our sky shortly before we took up space jumping ourselves. Sure, most of the reports were phonies. But some weren't. You have to believe evidence when you have it in front of you, or else the universe is just too fantastic. Surely you don't think that human beings are the only ones who ever built star ships?"

"Well . . . maybe not. But if somebody else has, why haven't they visited us long ago?"

"Simple arithmetic, pal; it's a big universe and we're just one small corner of it. Or maybe they did. That's my own notion; they surveyed us and Earth wasn't what they wanted —maybe us, maybe the climate. So the U.F.O.'s went away." He considered it. "Maybe they landed just long enough to fuel."

That was all I got out of my tenure as a member of the scientific party; when Harry submitted my name on his list, the Captain drew a line through it. "No special communicators will leave the ship."

That settled it; the Captain had a will of iron. Van got to go, as his brother had been killed in an accident while we were at peak—so I called Pat and told him about Van and suggested that Pat drop dead. He didn't see anything funny in it.

The *Elsie* landed in ocean comfortably deep, then they used the auxiliaries to bring her close to the shore. She floated high out of the water, as two-thirds of her tank were empty, burned up, the water completely disintegrated in boosting us first up to the speed of light, then backing u down again. The engineers were already overhauling he torch before we reached final anchorage. So far as I know none of them volunteered for the landing party; I think tha to most of the engineers the stop on Constance was just chance to pick up more boost mass and take care of repairs and overhauls they had been unable to do while under-way. They didn't care where they were or where they were going so long as the torch worked and all the machinery ticked. Dr. Devereaux told me that the Staff Metallurgist had been out to Pluto six times and had never set foot on any planet but Earth.

"Is that normal?" I asked, thinking how fussy Doc had been about everybody else, including me.

"For his breed of cat, it's robust mental health. Any other breed I would lock up and feed through the keyhole."

Sam Rojas was as annoyed as I was at the discrimination against us telepaths; he had counted on planting his feet on strange soil, like Balboa and Columbus and Lundy. He came around to see me about it. "Tom, are you going to stand for it?"

"Well, I don't want to—but what can we *do?*"

"I've been talking to some of the others. It's simple. We don't."

"We don't what?"

"Mmm . . . we just don't. Tom, ever since we slowed down, I've detected a falling off in my telepathic ability. It seems to be affecting all of us—those I've talked to. How about yourself?"

"Why, I haven't—"

"Think hard," he interrupted. "Surely you've noticed it. Why, I doubt if I could raise my twin right now. It must have something to do with where we are . . . maybe there is something odd about the radiation of Tau Ceti, or some-thing. Or maybe it comes from Connie. Who knows? And, for that matter, who can check on us?"

I began to get the pattern. I didn't answer, because it was a tempting idea.

"If we can't communicate," he went on, "we ought to be useful for something else . . . like the landing party, for in-stance. Once we are out of range of this mysterious in-fluence probably we would be able to make our reports back to Earth all right. Or maybe it would turn out that some of the girls who didn't want to go with the landing party could

123

manage to get in touch with Earth and carry the reports
... provided us freaks weren't discriminated against."

"It's an idea," I admitted.

"Think about it. You'll find your special talent getting
weaker and weaker. Me, I'm stone deaf already." He went
away.

I toyed with the idea. I knew the Captain would recognize a strike when he saw one . . . but what could he
do? Call us all liars and hang us by our thumbs until we
gave in? How could he be certain that we hadn't all gone
sour as m-r's? The answer was that he could not be certain;
nobody but a mind reader knows what it feels like, nobody
but the mind reader himself can tell that he is doing it. When
we slipped out of contact at peak he hadn't doubted us, he
had just accepted it. He would have to accept it now, no
matter what he thought.

For he had to have us; we were indispensable.

Dad used to be arbitration representative in his guild
local; I remembered his saying once that the only strike worth
calling was one in which the workers were so badly needed
that the strike would be won before a walkout. That was
the pinch we had the Captain in; he *had* to have us. No
strikebreakers closer than eleven light-years. He wouldn't
dare get rough with us.

Except that any one of us could break the strike. Let's
see—Van was out of it and so was Cas Warner; they were
no longer telepaired, their twins were dead. Pru's sister
Patience was still alive, but that telepair had never been
mended after peak—her sister had refused the risky drugs and
hypnosis routine and they never got back into rapport. Miss
Gamma did not count, because the ships her two sisters were
in were still peaking, so we were cut off from sidewise relay
back to Earth until one of them decelerated. Not counting
Sam and myself, whom did that leave? And could they be
counted on? There was Rupe, Gloria, Anna, and Dusty . . .
and Unc of course. And Mei-Ling.

Yes, they were solid. Making us feel that we were freaks
when we first came aboard had consolidated us. Even if one
or two didn't feel right about it, nobody would let the other

124

down. Not even Mei-Ling who was married to an outsider. It would work. If Sam could line them up.

I wanted to go dirtside the worst way . . . and maybe this was the worst way, but I still wanted to.

Just the same, there was something sneaky about it, like a kid spending his Sunday School collection money.

Sam had until noon the next day to get it lined up, because we were down to one watch a day. A continuous communication watch was not necessary and there was more ship's work to do now that we were getting ready to explore. I tabled the matter and went down to tag the rats that would be used by the scientific survey.

But I did not have to wait until the following day; Unc called us together that evening and we crowded into his room—all but Miss Gamma and Van and Pru and Cas. Unc looked around, looking horse-faced and sad, and said he was sorry we couldn't all sit down but he wouldn't keep us long. Then he started a meandering speech about how he thought of us all as his children and he had grown to love us and we would always be his children, no matter what. Then he started talking about the dignity of being a human being.

"A man pays his bills, keeps himself clean, respects other people, and keeps his word. He gets no credit for this; he has to do this much just to stay even with himself. A ticket to heaven comes higher."

He paused and added, "Especially he keeps his promises." He looked around and added, "That's all I had to say. Oh, I might as well make one announcement while we are here. Rupe has had to shift the watch list around a little bit." He picked out Sam Rojas with his eyes. "Sam, I want you to take next watch, tomorrow noon. Will you do it?"

There wasn't a sound for about three heart beats. Then Sam said slowly, "Why, I guess so, Unc, if you want me to."

"I'd be much obliged, Sam. One way and another, I don't want to put anybody else on that watch . . . and I wouldn't feel like standing it myself if you couldn't do it. I guess I would just have to tell the Captain there wasn't anybody available. So I'm pleased that you'll do it."

"Uh, why, sure, Unc. Don't worry about it."

And that was the end of the strike.

Unc didn't let us go quite yet. "I thought I'd tell you about the change in the watch list while I had you here and save Rupe from having to take it around to have you initial it. But I called you together to ask you about something else. The landing party will be leaving the ship before long. Nice as Constance looks, I understand that it will be risky . . . diseases that we don't know about, animals that might turn out to be deadly in ways we didn't expect, almost anything. It occurred to me that we might be able to help. We could send one of us with the landing party and keep one of us on watch in the ship—and we could arrange for their telepairs to relay by telephone. That way we'd always be in touch with the landing party, even if radios broke down or no matter what. It would be a lot of extra work and no glory . . . but it would be worth it if it saved the life of one shipmate."

Sam said suddenly, "Who are you figuring on to go with the landing party, Unc?"

"Why, I don't know. It isn't expected of us and we don't rate special-hazard pay, so I wouldn't feel like *ordering* anybody—I doubt if the Captain would back me up. But I was hoping for enough volunteers so that we could rotate the dirtside watch." He blinked and looked unsure of himself. "But nobody is expected to volunteer. I guess you had better let me know privately."

He didn't have to wait; we all volunteered. Even Mei-Ling did and then got mad and cried when Unc pointed out gently that she had better have her husband's consent—which she wasn't going to get; the Travers family was expecting a third.

Unc tackled the Captain the next morning. I wanted to hang around and hear the outcome but there was too much work to do. I was surprised, a half hour later, to be paged by speaker down in the lab; I washed my hands and hurried up to the Old Man's cabin.

Unc was there, looking glum, and the Captain was looking stern. I tried to call Unc on the Sugar-Pie band, t find out where things stood, but for once he ignored me. The Captain looked at me coldly and said, "Bartlett, Mr. McNeil has proposed a plan whereby the people in your department want to help out in the dirtside survey. I'll tell you right off that I have turned it down. The offer is appreciated—but I have no more intention of risking people in your special category in such duty than I would approve of modifying the ship's torch to sterilize the dinner dishes. First things first!"

He drummed on his desk. "Nevertheless, the suggestion has merit. I won't risk your whole department . . . but I might risk one special communicator to increase the safeguards for the landing party. Now it occurred to me that we have one sidewise pair right in this ship, without having to relay through Earth. You and Mr. McNeil. Well? What have you to say?"

I started to say, "Sure!"—then thought frantically. If I got to go after all that had happened, Sam was going to take a very dark view of it . . . and so was everybody. They might think I had framed it.

"Well? Speak up!"

Doggone, no matter what they thought, it wasn't a thing you could refuse. "Captain, you know perfectly well I volunteered for the landing party several days ago."

"So you did. All right, I'll take your consent for granted. But you misunderstood me. You aren't going; that will be Mr. McNeil's job. You'll stay here and keep in touch with him."

I was so surprised that I almost missed the next thing the Captain said. I shot a remark to Unc privately: ("What's this, Unc? Don't you know that all of them will think you swindled them?")

This time he answered me, distress in his voice: *"I know it, son. He took me by surprise."*

("Well, what are you going to do?")

"I don't know. I'm wrong both ways."

Sugar Pie suddenly cut in with, *"Hey! What are you two fussing about?"*

Unc said gently: *"Go away, honey. This is man talk."*

"Well!" But she didn't interrupt again. Perhaps she listened.

The Captain was saying: "—in any doubly-manned position, we will never risk the younger when the elder can serve. That is standard and applies as much to Captain Urqhardt and myself as it does to any other two. The mission comes first. Bartlett, your expected usefulness is at least forty years longer than that of Mr. McNeil. Therefore he must be preferred for a risk task. Very well, gentlemen. You'll receive instructions later."

("Unc—what are you going to tell Sam? Maybe *you* agree—I don't!")

"Don't joggle my elbow, son." He went on aloud: "No, Captain."

The Captain stared. "Why, you old scoundrel! Are you that fond of your skin?"

Unc faced him right back. "It's the only one I have, Captain. But that doesn't have anything to do with the case. And maybe you were a little hasty in calling me names."

"Eh?" The Captain turned red. "I'm sorry, McNeil. I take that back. But I think you owe me an explanation for your attitude."

"I'm going to give it, sir. We're old men, both of us. I can get along without setting foot on this planet and so can you. But it looks different to young people. You know perfectly well that my people volunteered for the landing party not because they are angels, not scientists, not philanthropists . . . but because they are aching to go ashore. You know that; you told me as much, not ten minutes ago. If you are honest with yourself, you know that most of these children would never have signed up for this trip if they had suspected that they were to be locked up, never permitted to have what they call an 'adventure.' They didn't sign up for money; they signed up for the far horizons. Now you rob them of their reasonable expectations."

The Captain looked grim. He clenched and unclenched a fist, then said, "There may be something in what you say. But I must make the decisions; I can't delegate that. My decision stands. You go and Bartlett stays."

I said: ("Tell him he won't get a darn' message through!")

Unc didn't answer me. "I'm afraid not, Captain. This is a volunteer job . . . and I'm not volunteering."

The Captain said slowly, "I'm not sure that volunteering is necessary. My authority to define a man's duty is broad. I rather think you are refusing duty."

"Not so, Captain. I didn't say I wouldn't take your orders; I just said I was not volunteering. But I'd ask for written orders, I think, and I would endorse them: 'Accepted under protest,' and ask to have a copy transmitted to the Foundation. I don't volunteer."

"But—confound it, man! You volunteered with the rest. That's what you came in here for. And I picked you."

Unc shook his head. "Not quite, Captain. We volunteered as a group. You turned us down as a group. If I gave you the impression that I was volunteering any other way, I am sorry . . . but that's how it is. Now if you will excuse me, sir, I'll go back and tell my people you won't have us."

The Captain turned pink again. Then he suddenly started to roar with laughter. He jumped up and put his arm around Unc's narrow shoulders. "You old scoundrel! You *are* an old scoundrel, a mutinous black-hearted scoundrel. You make me long for the days of bread-and-water and the rope's end. Now sit back down and we'll work this out. Bartlett, you can go."

I left, reluctantly, and then stayed away from the other freaks because I didn't want to answer questions. But Unc was thoughtful; he called me, mind to mind, as soon as he was out of the Captain's cabin and told me the upshot. It was a compromise. He and I and Rupe and Sam would rotate, with the first trick (considered to be the most dangerous) to be his. The girls would take the shipside watch, with Dusty classed with them because of age. But a bone was thrown to them: once medicine and research classed the planet as safe, they would be allowed sightseeing, one at a time. "*I had to twist his arm on that part,*" Unc admitted, "*but he agreed.*"

Then it turned out to be an anticlimax; Connie was about

as dangerous as Kansas. Before any human went outside the ship other than encased in a quarantine suit we exposed rats and canaries and hamsters to natural atmosphere; they loved it. When the first party went ashore, still in quarantine suits but breathing Connie's air after it had passed through electrostatic precipitators, two more experimental animals went with them—Bernhard van Houten and Percival the Pig.

Van had been down in the dumps ever since his twin was killed; he volunteered and I think Dr. Devereaux urged the Captain to let him. Somebody had to do it; you can make all the microscopic and chemical tests you like—the day comes when a living man has to expose his skin to a planet to find out if it is friendly. As Dr. Babcock says, eventually you must climb the tree. So Van went ashore without a quarantine suit, wearing shorts and shirt and shoes and looking like a scoutmaster.

Percival the Pig did not volunteer, but he thought it was a picnic. He was penned in natural bush and allowed to forage, eating anything from Connie's soil that he thought was fit to eat. A pig has advantages as an experimental animal; he eats anything, just as rats and men do, and I understand that his metabolism is much like ours—pigs even catch many of the same diseases. If Percival prospered, it was almost certain that we would, particularly as Percy had not been given the inoculations that we had, not even the wide-spectrum G.A.R. serum which is supposed to give some protection even against diseases mankind has never encountered before.

Percy got fat, eating anything and drinking brook water. Van got a sunburn and then tanned. Both were healthy and the pioneer party took off their quarantine suits. Then almost everybody (even Percy) came down with a three-day fever and a touch of diarrhea, but everybody recovered and nobody caught it twice.

They rotated after that and all but Uncle Steve and Harry and certain ones whom they picked swapped with someone in the ship. Half of the second party were inoculated with serum made from the blood of those who had recovered from three-day fever; most of those did not catch it. But the ones who returned were not allowed back in the ship at once; they were quarantined on a temporary deck rigged above the top bulge of the *Elsie*.

I don't mean to say that the planet was just like a city park—you can get killed, even in Kansas. There was a big, lizardlike carnivore who was no bargain. One of those got Lefty Gomez the first time our people ran into one and the beast would have killed at least two more if Lefty had been the kind of man who insists on living forever. I would never have figured Lefty as a hero—he was assistant pastry cook and dry-stores keeper back in the ship—but Uncle Steve says that ultimate courage is the commonest human virtue and that seven out of ten are Medal of Honor men, given the circumstances.

Maybe so. I must be one of the other three. I don't think I would have stood my ground and kept poking away at the thing's eyes, armed only with a campfire spit.

But *tyrannosaurus ceti* was not dangerous enough to give the planet a down check, once we knew he was there and what he was. Any big cat would have been much more dangerous, because cats are smart and he was stupid. You had to shoot first, but an explosive bullet made him lie down and be a rug. He had no real defense against men and someday men would exterminate him.

The shore party camped within sight of the ship on the edge of beautiful Babcock Bay, where we were anchored. The two helicopters patrolled each day, always together so that one could rescue the men in the other if it went down, and never more than a few hundred miles from base. Patrols on foot never went more than ten miles from base; we weren't trying to conquer the country, but simply trying to find out if men could conquer and hold it. They could . . . at least around Babcock Bay . . . and where men can get a toe hold they usually hang on.

My turn did not come until the fourth rotation and by then they were even letting women go ashore; the worry part was over.

The oddest thing about being outdoors was the sensation of weather; I had been in air-conditioning for two years and

131

I had forgotten rain and wind and sunshine in your face. Aboard the *Elsie* the engineer on watch used to cycle the temperature and humidity and ozone content on a random schedule, which was supposed to be good for our metabolisms. But it wasn't weather; it was more like kissing your sister.

The first drop of rain I felt startled me; I didn't know what it was. Then I was running up and down and dancing like a kid and trying to catch it in my mouth. It was rain, real rain and it was wonderful!

I couldn't sleep that night. A breeze on my face and the sounds of others sleeping around me and the distant noises of live things outside our snooper fences and the lack of perfect darkness all kept me awake. A ship is alive, too, and has its noises, but they are different from those outdoors; a planet is alive in another way.

I got up quietly and tip-toed outside. In front of the men's quarters about fifty feet away I could see the guardsman on watch. He did not notice me, as he had his head bent over dials and displays from the inner and outer fences and from the screen over us. I did not want to talk, so I went around behind the hut, out of sight of even the dim light from his instruments. Then I stopped and looked up.

It was the first good view of the sky I had had since we had left Earth and the night was clear. I stood there, dazzled and a little drunk from it.

Then I started trying to pick out constellations.

It was not hard; eleven light-years is just down the street for most stars. The Dipper was overhead, looking a little more battered than it does from Earth but perfectly recognizable. Orion blazed near the horizon ahead of me but Procyon had moved over a long way and Sirius was not even in sight—skidded below the skyline, probably, for Sirius is even closer to the Earth than is Tau Ceti and our position would shift him right across the sky. I tried to do a spherical triangle backwards in my head to figure where to look for Sirius and got dizzy and gave up.

Then I tried to find Sol. I knew where he would be, in

Boötes, between Arcturus and Virgo—but I had to find Boötes, before I could look for Father Sol.

Boötes was behind me, as close to the skyline as Orion was on the other side. Arcturus had shifted a little and spoiled the club shape of Boötes but there was no doubt in my mind.

There it was! A yellow-white star, the color of Capella, but dimmer, about second magnitude, which was right, both position and magnitude. Besides, it had to be the Sun, because there hadn't been any star that bright in that location when Pat and I were studying for our astrogation merit badge. It was the Sun.

I stared at it, in a thoughtful melancholy, warm rather than sad. I wondered what Pat was doing? Walking the baby, maybe. Or maybe not; I couldn't remember what the Greenwich ought to be. There he was, thirty years old and a couple of kids, the best part of his life behind him . . . and here I was, just old enough to be finishing my sophomore year in college if I were home.

No, I wouldn't be; I'd be Pat's age.

But I *wasn't* thirty.

I cheered up and decided that I had the best break after all, even if it had seemed not so good at first. I sighed and walked around a bit, not worrying, for not even one of those lizard brutes could get close to our night defenses without bringing thunder and lightning down around his ears. If he had ears. Percy's pen was not far in that rear direction; he heard me and came to his fence, so I walked up and scratched his snout. "Nice place, eh, boy?" I was thinking that when the *Elsie* did get home—and I no longer believed Uncle Steve's dire predictions—when I did get back, I would still be in my early twenties, just a good age to emigrate. And Connie looked like a fine place to come back to.

Percy answered with a snuffling grunt which I interpreted to mean: "You didn't bring me anything to eat? A fine way to treat a pal!" Percy and I were old friends; aboard ship I fed him, along with his brothers and the hamsters and the rats.

"Percy, you're a pig."

He did not argue but continued to snuffle into my empty hand. I was thinking that eleven light-years wasn't far; it was about right. The stars were still familiar.

Presently Percy got tired of it and so did I, so I wiped my hand on my pants and went back to bed.

XIII   IRRELEVANT RELATIONS

Beyond Beta Hydri: I ought to bring this up to date, or else throw it away. I hardly ever have time to write now, since we are so short handed. Whatever it was we picked up on Constance—or, possibly, caught from improperly fumigated stores—has left us with more than enough to do, especially in my department. There are only six left now to handle all the traffic, Unc, myself, Mei-Ling, Anna, Gloria, and Sam. Dusty lived through it but he is out of touch, apparently permanently. His brother had no kids for a secondary team and they just slipped apart on the last peak and never matched in again.

I am dependent on my great-niece Kathleen and on Molly, her mother. Pat and I can still talk, but only with their help; if we try it alone, it's like trying to make yourself understood in a machine shop. You know the other fellow is saying something but the more you strain the less you hear. Pat is fifty-four, now that we have peaked on this leg; we just don't have anything in common. Since Maude's death he isn't interested in anything but business—and I am not interested in that.

Unc is the only one who doesn't feel his original telepartner slipping away. Celestine is forty-two now; they are coming together instead of separating. I still call her "Sugar Pie," just to hear her chuckle. It is hard to realize that she is twice my age; she ought to have braids and a missing front tooth.

All in all, we lost thirty-two people in the Plague. I had it and got well. Doc Devereaux didn't get well and neither did Prudence nor Rupe. We have to fill in and act as if the others had never been with us. Mei-Ling's baby died and for a while we thought we were going to lose Mei-Ling, but now she takes her watch and does her work and even laughs. I guess the one we all miss the most is Mama O'Toole.

What else of importance has happened? Well, what can happen in a ship? Nothing. Beta Hydri was a washout. Not only nothing resembling an Earth-type planet, but no oceans —no water oceans, I mean; it was a choice for fuel between ammonia and methane, and the Chief Engineer and the Captain had long worried conferences before they settled for ammonia. Theoretically the *Elsie* will burn anything; give her mass-converter something to chew on and the old "e equals mc^2" gets to work; the torch spits the mass out as radiation at the speed of light and neutrons at almost the speed of light. But while the converter does not care, all of the torch's auxiliary equipment is built to handle fluid, preferably water.

We had a choice between ammonia, already liquid, and an outer planet that was mostly ice, but ice not much warmer than absolute zero. So they crossed their fingers, put her down in an ocean of ammonia, and filled up the old girl's tanks. The planet we named Inferno and then called it nastier names. We had to sit there four days at two gravities and it was cold, even with the ship's air heaters going full blast.

The Beta Hydri system is one I am not going back to; creatures with other metabolisms can have it and welcome. The only one who was pleased was Harry Gates, because the planetary arrangements followed Bode's Law. I wouldn't care if they had been in Vee formation.

The only other thing that sticks in my mind was (of all things!) political trouble. Our last peak started just as that war broke out between the Afro-European Federation and Estados Unidos de Sud. It shouldn't have meant anything to us—it did not, to most of us, or at least we kept our sympathies to ourselves. But Mr. Roch, our Chief Engineer, is from the Federation and his first assistant was born in Buenos Aires. When Buenos Aires got it, probably including some of Mr. Regato's relatives, he blamed his boss personally. Silly, but what can you expect?

After that, the Captain gave orders that he would check Earthside news before it was printed and he reminded us of the special restrictions on communicators in re security of communications. I think I would have been bright enough to submit that dispatch to the Captain before printing it, but I can't be sure. We'd had always had free press in the *Elsie*.

The only thing that got us out of that mess was that we peaked right after. When we came out of peak, fourteen years had passed and the latest political line-up had Argentina friends with her former enemies and on the outs with the rest of South America. After a while Mr. Roch and Mr. Regato were back playing chess together, just as if the Captain had never had to restrict them to keep them from each other's throats.

Everything that happens back on Earth is a little unreal to me, even though we continue to get the news when we are not at peak. You get your mind adjusted to a new situation; the *Elsie* goes through a peak . . . years have passed and everything has changed. They are calling the Planetary League the "United System" now and they say that the new constitution makes war impossible.

It's still the Planetary League to me—and it was supposed to make war impossible, too. I wonder what they changed besides the names?

Half of the news I don't understand. Kathleen tells me that her class has pooled their eveners to buy a Fardie for their school as a graduation present and that they are going to outswing it for the first time at the commencement exercises—then she had to hurry away because she had been co-opted in charge. That was just last watch. Now what is a "Fardie" and what was wrong with it where it was?

The technical news that reaches us I don't understand, either, but at least I know why and usually somebody aboard does understand it. The relativists are excited about stuff coming in which is so technical that it has to be retransmitted and confirmed before it is released—this with Janet Meers standing behind you and trying to snatch spools out of the recorder. Mr. O'Toole gets excited too, only the way he shows it is for the end of his nose to get pink. Dr. Babcock never shows excitement, but he missed coming in for meals two days running after I copied a monograph called "Sumner on Certain Aspects of Irrelevance." At the end of that time I sent one back to LRF which Dr. Babcock had written. It was just as crammed with indigestible mathematics, but I gathered that Dr. Babcock was politely calling Professor Sumner a fool.

Janet Meers tried to explain it to me, but all that I got out of it was that the concept of simultaneity was forcing a complete new look at physics.

"Up to now," she told me, "we've concentrated on the relative aspects of the space-time continuum. But what you m-r people do is *irrelevant* to space-time. Without time there is no space; without space there can be no time. Without space-time there can be no conservation of energy-mass. Heavens, there's *nothing*. It has driven some of the old-timers out of their minds. But now we are beginning to see how you people may possibly fit into physics—the new physics, I mean; it's all changed."

I had had enough trouble with the old-style physics; having to learn a new one made my head ache just to think about it. "What use is it?" I asked.

She looked shocked. "Physics doesn't have to have any *use*. It just *is*."

"Well, I don't know. The old physics was useful. Take the torch that drives us, for example—"

"Oh, that! That's not physics, that's just engineering"— as if I had mentioned something faintly scandalous.

I will never understand Janet and perhaps it is just as well that she promised to "be a sister to me." She said that she did not mind my being younger than she was, but that she did not think she could look up to a man who could not solve a fourth-degree function in his head. ". . . and a wife should always look up to her husband, don't you think?"

We were making the boosts at 1.5 gravity now. What with slippage, it cuts each up-boost and each down-boost to about four months, S-time, even though the jumps are longer. During boost I weigh 220 pounds and I've started wearing arch supports, but 50% extra weight is all right and is probably good for us, since it is too easy not to get enough exercise aboard ship.

The LRF has stopped using the drug stuff to help communication at peak, which would have pleased Dr. Devereaux since he disapproved of it so. Now your telepartner patches in with the help of hypnosis and suggestion alone, or you don't patch. Kathleen managed to cross the last peak with me that way, but I can see that we are going to lose communication teams all through the fleet, especially those who have not managed to set up tertiary telepartners. I don't know where my own team would be without Kathleen. In the soup, I guess. As it is, the *Niña* and the *Henry Hudson* are each down to two teams and the other four ships still in contact with Earth are not much better off. We are probably in the best shape, although we don't get much fleet news since Miss Gamma fell out of step with her sisters—or lost them, as the case may be; the *Santa Maria* is listed as "missing" but the *Marco Polo* is simply carried as "out of contact" as she was approaching peak when last heard from and won't be out of it for several Greenwich years.

We are headed now for a little G-type star so dim from Earth that it doesn't rate a name, nor even a Greek-letter constellation designation, but just a catalog number. From Earth it lies in Phoenix, between Hydrus the Sea Serpent and Cetus the Whale. ("Hydrus," not "Hydra"—Hydra is six R.A. hours over and farther north.) Unc called it a "Whistle Stop" so that is what we dubbed it, because you can't reel off a Palomar Catalog number each time you speak of where you are going. No doubt it will get an impressive name if it turns out to have a planet half as good as Connie. Incidentally, Connie will be colonized in spite of the epidemic we may have picked up there; the first shiploads are on their way. Whatever the bug was that bit us (and it very possibly may have come from Earth), it is no worse than half a dozen other diseases men have had and have fought back at and licked. At least, that is the official view and the pioneer ships are going on the assumption that they will probably catch it and have to conquer it.

Personally, I figure that one way of dying is as dangerous as another; when you're dead, you're dead—even if you die from "nothing serious." And the Plague, bad as it was, didn't kill me.

"Whistle Stop" wasn't worth a stop. We're on our way to Beta Ceti, sixty-three light-years from Earth.

I wish Dusty were still hooked up to transmit pictures; I would like one of my great-grandniece Vicky. I know what she looks like—carroty red hair, freckles across her nose, green eyes, a big mouth and braces on her teeth. At present she is sporting a black eye as well, picked up at school when somebody called her a freak and she resented it—I would love to have seen that fight! Oh, I know what she looks like but I'd like a picture anyhow.

It is funny how our family has run to girls. No, when I add it up, counting all descendants of my sisters as well as my brother, it comes out about even. But Maude and Pat had two girls and no boys, and I went away and did not get married, so the Bartlett name has died out.

I certainly would like to have a picture of Vicky. I know she is homely, but I'll bet she is cute, too—the kind of tomboy who always has scabs on her knees because she won't play the ladylike games. She generally hangs around for a while after we are through transmitting and we talk. Probably she is just being polite, for she obviously thinks of me as being as old as her great-grandfather Bartlett even though her mother has told her that I am not. I suppose it depends on where you sit. I ought to be in my last year in college now, but she knows that I am Pat's twin.

If she wants to put a long white beard on me, that is all

right with me, for the sake of her company. She was in a hurry this morning but nice about it. *"Will you excuse me, please, Uncle Tom? I've got to go study for a quiz in algebra."*

("Realio trulio?") I said.

"Realio trulio, cross my heart. I'd like to stay."

("Run along, Freckle Face. Say hello to the folks.")

" 'Bye! I'll call you a little early tomorrow."

She really is a nice child.

XIV   ELYSIA

Beta Ceti is a big star in the main spectral sequence, almost big enough to be classed as a giant—a small giant, thirty-seven times as bright as the Sun. It looks so bright from Earth that it has a name of its own, Deneb Kaitos, but we never call it that because "Deneb" brings to mind the other Deneb, Alpha Cygni, which is a real giant in a different part of the sky almost sixteen hundred light-years away.

Since Beta Ceti is so much brighter than the Sun, the planet we had been looking for, if it existed at all, had to be nearly six hundred million miles out, farther than Jupiter is from Sol.

We've found one, at five hundred and eighty million miles, which is close enough. Better yet, it is the smallest planet in a system that seems to run to outsizes; the one in the next track beyond is bigger than Jupiter.

I scheduled most of the routine skyside survey of Elysia, under Harry Gates' absentminded supervision. Harry is as eager as a fox terrier to finish his *magnum opus* before he has to knock off and take charge of the ground survey. He wants to transmit it back Earthside and preserve his name in science's hall of fame—not that he puts it that way, for Harry isn't stuck up; nevertheless, he thinks he has worked out a cosmogony for solar systems which includes Bode's Law. He says that if he is right, any star in the main spectral sequence will have planets.

Maybe . . . I would not know. But I can't see what use a star is without planets and I don't believe all this complicated universe got here by accident. Planets are meant to be used.

Acting as Harry's Man Friday has not been difficult. All I had to do was to dig the records of the preliminary survey of Connie out of the microfilms and write up similar schedules for Elysia, modified to allow for our loss of personnel. Everybody was eager to help, because (so far as we know) we are the only ship to draw a lucky number twice and only one of four to hit even once. But we are down now, water-borne, and waiting for medicine to okay Elysia for ground survey; I'm not quite so rushed. I tried to get in touch with Vicky and just chat this evening. But it happens to be evening back home, too, and Vicky is out on a date and politely put me off.

Vicky grew up some when we peaked this last jump; she now takes notice of boys and does not have as much time for her ancient uncle. ("Is it George?") I asked when she wanted to know if my call was important.

"Well, if you must know, it is George!" she blurted out.

("Don't get excited, Freckle Face,") I answered. ("I just asked.")

"Well, I told you."

("Sure, sure. Have a good time, hon, and don't stay out too late.")

"You sound just like Daddy."

I suppose I did. The fact is I don't have much use for George, although I have never seen him, never will, and don't know much about him, except that Vicky says that he is "the tenth power" and "first with the worst" in spite of being "ruffily around the round" if I knew what she meant, but she would equalize that.

I didn't know what she meant, but I interpreted it to mean

approval slightly qualified and that she expected him to be perfect, or "ricketty all through" when she got through making him over. I suspect him of being the kind of pimply-faced, ignorant young bore that I used to be myself and have always disliked—something about like Dusty Rhodes at the present without Dusty's amazing mind.

This sounds as if I were jealous of a boy I'll never see over a girl I have never seen, but that is ridiculous. My interest is fatherly, or big-brotherly, even though I am effectively no relation to her; i.e., my parents were two of her sixteen great-great-grandparents—a relationship so distant that most people aren't even aware of relatives of that remote degree.

Or maybe Van's wild theory has something to it and we are all getting to be cranky old men—just our bodies are staying young. But that is silly. Even though seventy-odd Greenwich years have passed, it has been less than four for me since we left Earth. My true time is hunger and sleep; I've slept about fourteen hundred times in the *Elsie* and eaten three meals and a snack or two for each sleep. That is four years, not seventy.

No, I'm just disappointed that on my first free evening in a couple of weeks I have nothing better to do than write in my diary. But, speaking of sleep, I had better get some; the first party will go ashore tomorrow, if medicine approves, and I will be busy. I won't be on it but there is plenty to do to get them off.

We are a sorry mess. I don't know what we can do now. I had better begin at the beginning. Elysia checked out in all ways on preliminary survey—breathable atmosphere, climate within Earth limits and apparently less extreme; a water, oxygen and carbon dioxide life cycle; no unusual hazards. No signs of intelligent life, of course, or we would have skipped it. It is a watery world even more than Terra is, with over 90% oceans and there was talk of naming it "Aquaria" instead of Elysia, but somebody pointed out that there was no sense in picking a name which might make it unattractive to colonists when there seemed to be nearly as much usable land as Earth had.

So we cuddled up to an island as big as Madagascar—almost a continent for Elysia—with the idea that we could cover the whole island in the detailed survey and be able to report that a colony could settle there as fast as LRF could send a ship—we knew that Connie was already settled and we wanted to get this one settled and make it a clean sweep for the *Elsie*.

I gave Percy a pat and told him to size up the lay of the land and to let me know if he found any lady pigs. Uncle Lucas took the guard ashore and the science party followed the same day. It was clear that Elysia was going to be no more of a problem than Connie had been and almost as big a prize—except for the remote possbiility of exotic infection we could not handle.

That was two weeks ago.

It started out routine as breakfast. Percy and the other experimental animals flourished on an Elysian diet; Van failed to catch anything worse than an itch and presently he was trying Elysian food himself—there were awkward looking four-winged birds which broiled nicely; Van said they reminded him of roast turkey with an overtone of cantaloupe. But Percy the Pig would not touch some fish that were caught and the rats that did eat them died, so sea food was put off until further investigation could be made. The fish did not look like ours; they were flat the wrong way, like a flounder, and they had tendrils something like a catfish which ravelled on the ends instead of being spiny. Harry Gates was of the opinion that they were feeling organs and possibly manipulative as well.

The island had nothing like the big-mouthed carnivorous lizards that got Lefty Gomez. However, there was no telling what might be on other islands, since the land masses were so detached that totally different lines of evolution might have been followed in each island group. Our report was going to recommend that Devereaux Island be settled first, then investigate the others cautiously.

I was due to go ashore on third rotation, Unc having taken the first week, then a week of rest, and now would take shipside watch while I linked with him from ashore. But at the last minute I agreed to swap, as Anna was anxious to go. I did not want to swap, but I had been running the department's watch list since Rupe's death and it would have been awkward to refuse. Gloria was going, too, since her husband was on that rotation, but Gloria did not count as her telepartner was on vacation back Earthside.

When they left, I was on top of the *Elsie*, glumly watching them get into the boats. There was a "monkey island" deck temporarily rigged up there, outside the airlock; it was a good place to watch the boats being loaded at the cargo ports lower down. Engineering had completed inspection and overhaul and had about finished filling the boost-mass tanks; the *Elsie* was low in the water and the cargo ports were not more than ten feet above waterline. It made loading convenient; at the time we put the first party ashore the tanks were empty and the boats had to be lowered nearly a hundred feet and passengers had to go down rope ladders—not easy for people afraid of heights, as so many are. But it was a cinch that day.

The airlock was only large enough for people; anything bigger had to go through the cargo ports. It was possible to rig the cargo ports as airlocks and we had done so on Inferno around Beta Hydri, but when the air was okay we just used them as doors. They were at the cargo deck, underneath the mess deck and over the auxiliary machinery spaces; our three boats and the two helicopters were carried just inside on that deck. The boats could be swung out on gooseneck davits from where they nested but the helicopters had to be hooked onto boat falls, swung out, then a second set of falls hooked to them from the monkey island above, by which a helicopter could be scooted up the *Elsie*'s curved side and onto the temporary top deck, where her jet rotors would be attached.

Mr. Regato cursed the arrangement every time we used it. "Mechanical buffoonery!" was his name for it. "I've never seen a ship's architect who wasn't happy as soon as he had a pretty picture. He never stops to think that some poor fool is going to have to *use* his pretty picture."

As may be, the arrangement did let the helis be unloaded

with a minimum of special machinery to get out of order—which, I understand, was a prime purpose in refitting the ships for the Project. But that day the helicopters were outside and ready, one of them at camp and the other tied down near me on the monkey island. All we had to do was to load the boats.

The boats were whale boats molded of glass and teflon and made nonsinkable by plastic foam in all dead spaces. They were so tough that, while you might be able to bash one in, you could not puncture it with anything short of a drill or a torch, yet they were so light that four men could lift one that was empty. It did them no harm to drive them up onto a rocky beach, then they could be unloaded and easily dragged higher. They were driven by alcohol jets, just as the helis were, but they had oars and sails as well. We never used the oars although all the men had gone through a dry drill under my Uncle Steve's watchful eye.

The boats had come in the night before loaded with specimens for the research department; now they were going back with people who would replace those ashore. From the monkey island I could see, half a mile away, the people who were coming back, waiting on the beach for the boats. Two of the boats were lying off, waiting for the third; each had about eighteen people in it and a few bundles of things requisitioned by Harry Gates for his scientific uses ashore, as well as a week's supplies for the whole party.

I noticed a movement behind me, turned, and saw that it was the Old Man coming up the airlock hatch. "Good morning, Captain."

"Morning, Bartlett." He looked around. "Nice day."

"Yes, sir . . . and a nice place."

"It is indeed." He looked toward the shore. "I'm going to find *some* excuse to hit dirt before we leave here. I've been on steel too long."

"I don't see why not, sir. This place is friendly as a puppy. Not like Inferno."

"Not a bit." He turned away, so I did too; you don't press conversation on the Captain unless he wants it. The third boat was loaded now and cast loose; all three were

145

about fifty yards away and were forming a column to go in together. I waved to Gloria and Anna.

At each boat, a long, wet rope as thick as my waist came up out of the water, passed across it amidships and back into the water on the other side. I yelled, "Hey, Captain! *Look!*"

He turned. The boats rolled sideways and sank—they were *pulled* under. I heard somebody scream and the water was crowded with struggling bodies.

The Captain leaned past me at the rail and looked at the disaster. He said in an ordinary tone, "Can you start that chopper?"

"Uh, I think so, Captain." I was not a helicopter pilot but I knew how it worked.

"Then do it." He leaned far over and yelled, "*Get that cargo door closed!*" He turned and dived down the hatch. I caught a glimpse of what had made him yell as I turned to climb into the helicopter. It was another of those wet ropes slithering up the *Elsie*'s side toward the cargo port.

Starting the helicopter was more complicated than I had realized, but there was a check-off list printed on the instrument panel. I had fumbled my way down to "step four: start impeller" when I was pushed aside by Ace Wenzel, the torchman who was the regular pilot. Ace did something with both hands, the blades started to revolve, making shadows across our faces, and he yelled, "Cast her loose!"

I was shoved out the door as the Surgeon was climbing in; I fell four feet to the deck as the down blast hit me. I picked myself up and looked around.

There was nothing in the water, *nothing*. Not a body, not a person struggling to keep afloat, no sign of the boats. There was not even floating cargo although some of the packages would float. I knew: I had packed some of them.

Janet was standing next to me, shaking with dry sobs. I said stupidly, "What happened?"

She tried to control herself and said shakily, "I don't know. I saw one of them get Otto. It just . . . it just—" She started to bawl again and turned away.

There wasn't anything on the water, but now I saw that

there was something *in* the water, under it. From high up you can see down into water if it is fairly smooth; arranged around the ship in orderly ranks were things of some sort. They looked like whales—or what I think a whale would look like in water; I've never seen a whale.

I was just getting it through my confused head that I was looking at the creatures who had destroyed the boats when somebody yelled and pointed. On shore the people who were to return were still on the beach, but they were no longer alone—they were surrounded. The things had come ashore, on each side of them and had flanked them. I could not see well at that distance but I could see the sea creatures because they were so much bigger than we were. They didn't have legs, so far as I could tell, but it did not slow them down—they were *fast*.

And our people were being herded into the water.

There was nothing we could do about it, not *anything*. Under us we had a ship that was the end product of centuries of technical progress; its torch could destroy a city in the blink of an eye. Ashore the guard had weapons by which one man was equal to an army of older times and there were more such weapons somewhere in the ship. But at the time I did not even know where the armory was, except that it was somewhere in the auxiliary deck—you can live a long time in a ship and never visit all her compartments.

I suppose I should have been down in the auxiliary deck, searching for weapons. But what I did was stand there, frozen, with a dozen others, and watch it happen.

But somebody had been more alert than I had been. Two men came bursting up through the hatch; they threw down two ranger guns and started frantically to plug them in and break open packages of ammunition. They could have saved the effort; by the time they were ready to sight in on the enemy, the beach was as empty as the surface of the water. Our shipmates had been pushed and dragged under. The helicopter was hovering over the spot; its rescue ladder was down but there was no one on it.

The helicopter swung around over the island and across our camp site, then returned to the ship.

While it was moving in to touch down, Chet Travers hurried up the ladder. He looked around, saw me and said, "Tom, where's the Captain?"

"In the chopper."

"Oh." He frowned. "Well, give him this. Urgent. I've got to get back down." He shoved a paper at me and disappeared. I glanced at it, saw that it was a message form, saw who it was from, and grabbed the Captain's arm as he stepped out of the heli.

He shrugged me off. "Out of my way!"

"Captain, you've *got* to—it's a message from the island —from Major Lucas."

He stopped then and took it from me, then fumbled for his reading glasses, which I could see sticking out of a pocket. He shoved the dispatch form back at me before I could help him and said, "Read it to me, boy."

So I did. " 'From: Commander Ship's Guard—To: Commanding Officer *Lewis and Clark*—Oh nine three one—at oh nine oh five survey camp was attacked by hostile natives, believed to be amphibious. After suffering initial heavy losses the attack was beaten off and I have withdrawn with seven survivors to the hilltop north of the camp. We were forced to abandon survey craft number two. At time of attack, exchange party was waiting on beach; we are cut off from them and their situation is not known but must be presumed to be desperate.

" 'Discussion: The attack was intelligently organized and was armed. Their principal weapon appears to be a jet of sea water at very high pressure but they use also a personal weapon for stabbing and cutting. It must be assumed that they have other weapons. It must be conditionally assumed that they are as intelligent as we are, as well disciplined and possibly as well armed for the conditions. Their superior numbers give them a present advantage even if they had no better weapons.

" 'Recommendations: My surviving command can hold out where it is against weapons thus far encountered. It is therefore urgently recommended that immediate measures be limited to rescuing beach party. Ship should then b

148

placed in orbit until a plan can be worked out and weapons improvised to relieve my command without hazard to the ship.—S. Lucas, Commandant, oh nine three six.' "

The Captain took the message and turned toward the hatch without speaking. Nobody said anything although there were at least twenty of us crowded up there. I hesitated, then when I saw that others were going down, I pushed in and followed the Captain.

He stopped two decks down and went into the communications office. I didn't follow him, but he left the door open. Chet Travers was in there, bent over the gear he used to talk with the camp, and Commander Frick was leaning over him with a worried look on his face. The Captain said, "Get me Major Lucas."

Commander Frick looked up. "We're trying to, Captain. Transmission cut off while they were sending us a list of casualties."

The Captain chewed his lip and looked frustrated, then he said, "Keep trying," and turned. He saw me.

"Bartlett!"

"Yes, sir!"

"You have one of your people over there. Raise him."

I thought rapidly, trying to remember the Greenwich even as I was calling Vicky—if Vicky was home, she could get through on the direct line to LRF and they could hook her with Sam Rojas's telepartner and thence to Sam, and the Captain could talk to Uncle Steve on a four-link relay almost as fast as he could by radio. ("Vicky! Come in, Vicky! Urgent!")

"Yes. Uncle Tom? What is it? I was asleep."

Commander Frick said, "I don't think that will work, Captain. Rojas isn't on the list of survivors. He was scheduled for rotation; he must have been down at the beach."

Of course, of course! Sam would have been down at the beach—I had stood by and must have watched him being herded into the water!

"What is it, Uncle Tom?"

("Just wait, hon. Stay linked.")

"Then get me somebody else," the Captain snapped.

149

"There isn't anyone else, Captain," Frick answered. "Here's the list of survivors. Rojas was the only fr— the only special communicator we had ashore."

The Captain glanced at the list, said, "Pass the word for all hands not on watch to assemble in the mess room on the double." He turned and walked right through me. I jumped out of the way.

"What's the matter, Uncle Tom? You sound worried."

I tried to control my voice. ("It was a mistake, hon. Just forget it and try to get back to sleep. I'm sorry.")

"All right. But you still sound worried."

I hurried after the Captain. Commander Frick's voice was calling out the order over the ship's system as we hurried down the ladders, yet he was only a moment or two behind me in reaching the mess room. In a matter of seconds we were all there . . . just a handful of those who had left Earth—about forty. The Captain looked around and said to Cas Warner, "Is this all?"

"I think so, Captain, aside from the engineering watch."

"I left Travers on watch," added Frick.

"Very well." The Captain turned and faced us. "We are about to rescue the survivors ashore. Volunteers step forward."

We didn't step, we surged, all together. I would like to say that I was a split second ahead, because of Uncle Steve, but it wouldn't be true. Mrs. Gates was carrying young Harry in her arms and she was as fast as I was.

"Thank you," the Captain said stiffly. "Now will the women please go over there by the pantry so that I can pick the men who will go."

"Captain?"

"Yes, Captain Urqhardt?"

"I will lead the party."

"You'll do nothing of the sort, sir. I will lead. You will now take some women and go down and fetch what we need."

Urqhardt barely hesitated, then said, "Aye, aye, sir."

"That rule—our standing rule for risk—will apply to all of you. In doubly-manned jobs the older man will go. In other jobs, if the job can be dispensed with, the man will go; if it cannot be, the man will stay." He looked around. "Dr. Babcock!"

"Righto, Skipper!"

Mr. O'Toole said, "Just a moment, Captain. I am a widower and Dr. Babcock is much more—"

"Shut *up*."

"But—"

"Confound it, sir, must I debate every decision with every one of you? Must I remind you that every second counts? Get over there with the women."

Red-faced and angry Mr. O'Toole did as he was told. The Captain went on, "Mr. Warner. Mr. Roch. Dr. Severin—" Quickly he picked those he wanted, then waved the rest of us over toward the pantry.

Uncle Alfred McNeil tried to straighten his stooped shoulders. "Captain, you forgot me. I'm the oldest in my department."

The Captain's face softened just a hair. "No, Mr. McNeil, I didn't forget," he said quietly, "but the capacity of the chopper is limited—and we have seven to bring back. So I must omit you."

Unc's shoulders sagged and I thought he was going to cry, then he shuffled over away from the selected few. Dusty Rhodes caught my eye and looked smug and proud; he was one of the chosen. He still did not look more than sixteen and I don't think he had ever shaved; this was probably the first time in his life that he had ever been treated in all respects as a man.

In spite of the way the others had been shut off short I couldn't let it stand. I stepped forward again and touched the Captain's sleeve. "Captain . . . you've *got* to let me go! My uncle is over there."

I thought he was going to explode, but he caught himself. "I see your point. But you are a special communicator and we haven't any spare. I'll tell Major Lucas that you tried."

"But—"

"Now shut up and do as you are told—before I kick you

151

half across the compartment." He turned away as if I didn't exist.

Five minutes later arms had been issued and we were all crowding up the ladders to see them off. Ace Wenzel started the helicopter at idling speed and jumped out. They filed in, eight of them, with the Captain last. Dusty had a bandolier over each shoulder and a ranger gun in his hands; he was grinning excitedly. He threw me a wink and said, "I'll send you a postcard."

The Captain paused and said, "Captain Urqhardt."

"Yes, sir."

The Captain and the reserve captain conferred for a moment; I couldn't hear them and I don't think we were meant to hear. Then Captain Urqhardt said loudly, "Aye, aye, sir. It shall be done."

"Very good, sir." The Captain stepped in, slammed the door, and took the controls himself. I braced myself against the down blast.

Then we waited.

I alternated between monkey island and the comm office. Chet Travers still could not raise Uncle Steve but he was in touch with the heli. Every time I went top side I looked for the sea things but they seemed to have gone away.

Finally I came down again to the comm room and Chet was looking joyful. "They've got 'em!" he announced. "They're off the ground." I started to ask him about it but he was turning to announce the glad news over the ship's system; I ran up to see if I could spot the heli.

I saw it, near the hilltop, about a mile and a half away. It moved rapidly toward the ship. Soon we could see people inside. As it got closer someone opened a window on the side toward us.

The Captain was not really skilled with a helicopter. He tried to make a landing straight in but his judgment of wind was wrong and he had to swing on past and try again. The maneuver brought the craft so close to the ship that we could see the passengers plainly. I saw Uncle Steve and he saw me and waved; he did not call out, he just waved. Dusty Rhodes was beside him and saw me, too. He grinned and

waved and shouted, "Hey, Tom, I rescued your buddy!"
He reached back and then Percy's head and cloven fore-
hooves showed above the frame, with Dusty holding the pig
with one hand and pointing to him with the other. They
were both grinning.

"Thanks!" I yelled back. "Hi, Percy!"

The chopper turned a few hundred feet beyond the ship
and headed back into the wind.

It was coming straight toward the ship and would have
touched down soon when something came out of the water
right under it. Some said it was a machine—to me it looked
like an enormous elephant's trunk. A stream of water so
solid, hard, and bright that it looked like steel shot out of
the end of it; it struck a rotor tip and the heli staggered.

The Captain leaned the craft over and it slipped out of
contact. The stream followed it, smashed against the fuse-
lage and again caught a rotor; the heli tilted violently and
began to fall.

I'm not much in an emergency; it is hours later when I
figure out what I should have done. This time I acted without thinking. I dived down the ladder without hitting the
treads and was on down in the cargo deck almost at once.
The port of that side was closed, as it had been since the
Captain ordered it closed earlier; I slapped the switch and
it began to grind open. Then I looked around and saw what
I needed: the boat falls, coiled loosely on deck, not yet
secured. I grabbed a bitter end and was standing on the
port as it was still swinging down to horizontal.

The wrecked helicopter was floating right in front of me
and there were people struggling in the water. "Uncle Steve!"
I yelled "Catch!" I threw the line as far as I could.

I had not even seen him as I yelled. It was just the idea
that was in the top of my mind. Then I did see him, far
beyond where I had been able to throw the line. I heard him
call back, "Coming, Tom!" and he started swimming strongly toward the ship.

I was so much in a daze that I almost pulled the line in
to throw it again when I realized that I had managed to

153

throw far enough for some one. I yelled again. "Harry! Right behind you! Grab on!"

Harry Gates rolled over in the water, snatched at the line and got it. I started to haul him in.

I almost lost him as I got him to the ship's skin. One of his arms seemed almost useless and he nearly lost his grasp. But between us we managed to manhandle him up and into the port; we would not have made it if the ship had not been so low in the water. He collapsed inside and lay on his face, gasping and sobbing.

I jerked the fall loose from his still clenched hand and turned to throw it to Uncle Steve.

The helicopter was gone, Uncle Steve was gone, again the water was swept clean—except for Percy, who, with his head high out of water, was swimming with grim determination toward the ship.

I made sure that there were no other people anywhere in the water. Then I tried to think what I could do for Percy.

The poor little porkchop could not grab a line, that was sure. Maybe I could lasso him. I fumbled to get a slip knot in the heavy line. I had just managed it when Percy gave a squeal of terror and I jerked my head around just in time to see him pulled under the water.

It wasn't a mouth that got him. I don't think it was a mouth.

XV   "CARRY OUT HER MISSION!"

I don't know what I expected after the attack by the behemoths. We just wandered around in a daze. Some of us tried to look out from the monkey island deck until that spouter appeared again and almost knocked one of us off, then Captain Urqhardt ordered all hands to stay inside and the hatch was closed.

I certainly did not expect a message that was brought around after supper (if supper had been served; some made themselves sandwiches) telling me to report at once for heads-of-departments conference. "That's you, isn't it, Tom?" Chet Travers asked me. "They tell me Unc Alfred is on the sick list. His door is closed."

"I suppose it's me." Unc had taken it hard and was in bed with a soporific in him, by order of the one remaining medical man, Dr. Pandit.

"Then you had better shag up there."

First I went to Captain Urqhardt's room and found it dark, then I got smart and went to the Captain's cabin. The door was open and some were already around the table with Captain Urqhardt at the head. "Special communications department, sir," I announced myself.

"Sit down, Bartlett."

Harry came in behind me and Urqhardt got up and shut the door and sat down. I looked around, thinking it was a mighty funny heads-of-departments meeting. Harry Gates was the only boss there who had been such when we left Earth. Mr. Eastman was there instead of Commander Frick. Mama O'Toole was long dead but now Cas was gone too; ecology was represented by Mr. Krishnamurti who had merely been in charge of air-conditioning and hydroponics when we had left. Mr. O'Toole was there in place of Dr. Babcock, Mr. Regato instead of Mr. Roch. Sergeant Andreeli, who was also a machinist in engineering, was there in place of Uncle Steve and he was the only member of the ship's guard left alive—because he had been sent back to the ship with a broken arm two days earlier. Dr. Pandit sat where Dr. Devereaux should have been.

And myself of course but I was just fill-in; Unc was still aboard. Worst of all, there was Captain Urqhardt sitting where the Captain should have been.

Captain Urqhardt started in. "There is no need to detail

our situation; you all know it. We will dispense with the usual departmental reports, too. In my opinion our survey of this planet is as complete as we can make it with present personnel and equipment . . . save that an additional report must be made of the hazard encountered today in order that the first colonial party will be prepared to defend itself. Is there disagreement? Dr. Gates, do you wish to make further investigations here?"

Harry looked surprised and answered, "No, Captain. Not under the circumstances."

"Comment?" There was none. "Very well," Urqhardt continued. "I propose to shape course for Alpha Phoenicis. We will hold memorial services at nine tomorrow morning and boost at noon. Comment? Mr. O'Toole."

"Eh? Do you mean can we have the figures ready? I suppose so, if Janet and I get right on it."

"Do so, as soon as we adjourn. Mr. Regato?"

Regato was looking astounded. "I didn't expect this, Captain."

"It is short notice, but can your department be ready? I believe you have boost mass aboard."

"It isn't that, Captain. Surely, the torch will be ready. But I thought we would make one long jump for Earth."

"What led you to assume that?"

"Why, uh . . ." The new Chief Engineer stuttered and almost slipped out of P-L lingo into Spanish. "The shape we are in, sir. The engineering department will have to go on watch-and-watch, heel and toe. I can't speak for other departments, but they can't be in much better shape."

"No, you can't and I am not asking you to. With respect to your own department, is it mechanically ready?"

Regato swallowed. "Yes, sir. But people break down as well as machinery."

"Wouldn't you have to stand watch-and-watch to shape course for Sol?" Urqhardt did not wait for the obvious answer, but went on, "I should not have to say this. We are not here for our own convenience; we are here on an assigned mission . . . as you all know. Earlier today, just be fore Captain Swenson left, he said to me, 'Take charge of my ship, sir. Carry out her mission.' I answered, 'Aye, aye, sir.' Let me remind you of that mission: we were sent out to conduct the survey we have been making, with orders to continue the search as long as we were in communication with Earth—when we fell out of communication, we were free to return to Earth, if possible. Gentlemen, we are still in touch with Earth; our next assigned survey point is Alpha Phoenicis. Could anything be clearer?"

My thoughts were boiling up so that I hardly heard him. I was thinking: who does this guy think he is? Columbus? Or the Flying Dutchman? There were only a little over thirty of us left alive—in a ship that had started with two hundred. The boats were gone, the heli's were— I almost missed his next remark.

"Bartlett?"

"Sir?"

"What about your department?"

It dawned on me that *we* were the key department—us freaks. When *we* fell out of touch, he *had* to turn back. I was tempted to say that we had all gone deaf, but I knew I couldn't get away with it. So I stalled.

"As you pointed out, sir, we are in touch with Earth."

"Very well." His eyes turned toward Dr. Pandit.

"Just a moment, Captain," I insisted. "There's more to it."

"Eh? State it."

"Well, this next jump is about thirty years, isn't it? Greenwich, I mean."

"Of that order. Somewhat less."

" 'Of that order.' There are three special communicators left, myself, Unc—I mean Mr. McNeil—and Mei-Ling Travers. I think you ought to count Unc out."

"Why?"

"Because he has his original telepartner and she is now as old as he is. Do you think Unc will live another thirty years?"

"But it won't be thirty years for him—oh, sorry! I see your point. She would be well past a hundred if she lived at all. Possibly senile."

"Probably, sir. Or more likely dead."

"Very well, we won't count McNeil. That leaves two of you. Plenty for essential communication."

"I doubt it, sir. Mei-Ling is a poor bet. She has only a secondary linkage and her partner is over thirty, with no children. Based on other telepairs, I would say that it is most unlikely that they will stay in rapport through another peak ... not a thirty-year one."

"That still leaves yourself."

I thought suddenly that if I had the guts to jump over the side, they could all go home. But it was just a thought; when I die, it won't be suicide. "My own case isn't much better, sir. My telepartner is about—" I had to stop and count up, then the answer did not seem right. "—is about nineteen, sir. No kids. No chance of kids before we peak ... and I couldn't link in with a brand-new baby anyhow. She'll be fiftyish when we come out. So far as I know, there hasn't been a case in the whole fleet of bridging that long a period out of rapport."

He waited several moments before he answered. "Have you any reason to believe that it is impossible?"

"Well ... no, sir. But it is extremely unlikely."

"Hmm ... do you consider yourself an authority in theory of telepathy?"

"Huh? No, sir. I am just a telepath, that's all."

"I think he is probably right," put in Dr. Pandit.

"Are you an authority, Doctor?"

"Me, sir? As you know, my specialty is exotic pathology. But—"

"In that case, we will consult authorities Earthside. Perhaps they can suggest some way to improve our chances. Very probably, under the circumstances, the Foundation will again authorize use of drugs to reduce the possibility that our special communicators might fall out of touch during peak. Or something."

I thought of telling him that Vicky wasn't going to risk dangerous habit-forming drugs. Then I thought better of it; Pat had—and Vicky might.

"That is all, gentlemen. We will boost at noon tomorrow

Uh, one more thing . . . One of you implied that morale is not too high in the ship. That is correct and I am perhaps more aware of it than you are. But morale will shake down to normal and we will best be able to forget the losses we have suffered if we all get quickly back to work. I want only to add that you all, as senior officers of this ship, have most to do with morale by setting an example. I am sure that you will." He stood up.

I don't know how news travels in a ship but by the time I got down to the mess room everybody knew that we were boosting tomorrow . . . and not for home. It was buzz-buzz and yammer all over. I ducked out because I didn't want to discuss it; my thoughts were mixed. I thought the Captain was insisting on one more jump from which he couldn't possibly report his results, if any—and with a nice fat chance that none of us would ever get home. On the other hand I admired the firm way he faced us up to our obligations and brushed aside panic. He had guts.

So did the Flying Dutchman have guts—but at last report he was still trying to round the Cape and not succeeding. The Captain—Captain Swenson, I corrected—would not have been that bullheaded.

Or would he? According to Urqhardt, the last thing the Captain had said had been to remind Urqhardt that it was up to him to carry out the mission. All of us had been very carefully chosen (except us freaks) and probably the skipper and the relief skipper of each ship were picked primarily for bulldog stubbornness, the very quality that had kept Columbus going on and on when he was running out of water and his crew was muttering mutiny. I remembered Uncle Steve had once suggested as much.

I decided to go talk to Uncle Steve . . . then I remembered I couldn't and I really felt bad. When my parents had died, two peaks back, I had felt bad because I didn't feel as bad as I knew I should have felt. When it happened—or rather, by the time I knew about it—they were long dead, people I had not seen in a long time and just faces in a photograph. But Uncle Steve I had seen every day—I had seen *today*.

And I had been in the habit of kicking my troubles around with him whenever they were too much for me.

I felt his loss then, the delayed shock you get when you are hit hard. The hurt doesn't come until you pull yourself together and realize you're hit.

It was just as well that somebody tapped on my door then, or I would have bawled.

It was Mei-Ling and her husband, Chet. I invited them in and they sat down on the bed. Chet got to the point. "Tom, where do you stand on this?"

"On what?"

"This silly businesss of trying to go on with a skeleton crew."

"It doesn't matter where I stand," I said slowly. "I'm not running the ship."

"Ah, but you are!"

"Huh?"

"I don't mean quite that, but I do mean you can put a stop to the nonsense. Now, look, Tom, everybody knows what you told the Captain and—"

"Who's been talking?"

"Huh? Never mind. If it didn't leak from you, it probably did from everybody else present; it's common knowledge. What you told him made sense. What it comes down to is that Urqhardt is depending on you and you alone to keep him in touch with the home office. So you're the man with the stick. You can stop him."

"Huh? Now wait. I'm not the only one. Granted that he isn't counting on Unc—how about Mei-Ling?"

Chet shook his head. "Mei-Ling isn't going to 'think-talk' for him."

His wife said, "Now, Chet, I haven't said so."

He looked at her fondly. "Don't be super-stupid, my lovely darling. You know that there is no chance at all that you will be any use to him after peak. If our brave Captain Urqhardt hasn't got that through his head now, he will . . even if I have to explain to him in words of one syllable."

"But I *might* stay linked."

"Oh, no, you won't . . . or I'll bash your pretty head in. Our kids are going to grow up on Earth."

She looked soberly at him and patted his hand. The Travers's were not expecting again, but everybody knew they were hoping; I began to see why Chet was adamant . . . and I became quite sure that Mei-Ling would not link again after peak—not after her husband had argued with her for a while. What Chet wanted was more important to her than what the Captain wanted, or any abstract duty to a Foundation back on Earth.

Chet went on, "Think it over, Tom, and you will see that you can't let your shipmates down. To go on is suicidal and everybody knows it but the Captain. It's up to you."

"Uh, I'll think it over."

"Do that. But don't take too long." They left.

I went to bed but didn't sleep. The deuce of it was that Chet was almost certainly right . . . including the certainty that Mei-Ling would never patch in with her telepair after another peak, for she was beginning to slip even now. I had been transmitting mathematical or technical matter which would have fallen to her ever since last peak, because her linking was becoming erratic. Chet wouldn't have to bash her admittedly-pretty head in; she was falling out of touch.

On the other hand . . .

When I had reached "On the other hand" about eighteen times, I got up and dressed and went looking for Harry Gates; it occurred to me that since he was a head of department and present at the meeting, it was proper to talk to him about it.

He wasn't in his room; Barbara suggested that I try the laboratory. He was there, alone, unpacking specimens that had been sent over the day before. He looked up. "Well, Tom, how is it going?"

"Not too good."

"I know. Say, I haven't had a proper chance to thank you. Shall I write it out, or will you have it right off my chest?"

"Uh, let's take it for granted." I had not understood him

at first, for it is the simple truth that I had forgotten about pulling him out of the water; I hadn't had time to think about it.

"As you say. But I won't forget it. You know that, don't you?"

"Okay. Harry, I need advice."

"You do? Well, I've got it in all sizes. All of it free and all of it worth what it costs, I'm afraid."

"You were at the meeting tonight."

"So were you." He looked worried.

"Yes." I told him all that had been fretting me, then thought about it and told him all that Chet had said. "What am I to do, Harry? Chet is right; the chance of doing any good on another jump isn't worth it. Even if we find a planet worth reporting—a chance that is never good, based on what the fleet has done as a whole—even so, we almost certainly won't be able to report it except by going back, two centuries after we left. It's ridiculous and, as Chet says, suicidal, with what we've got left. On the other hand, the Captain is right; this is what we signed up for. The ship's sailing orders say for us to go on."

Harry carefully unpacked a package of specimens before he answered.

"Tommie, you should ask me an easy one. Ask me whether or not to get married and I'll tell you like a shot. Or anything else. But there is one thing no man can tell another man and that is where his duty lies. That you must decide for yourself."

I thought about it. "Doggone it, Harry, how do *you* feel about it?"

"Me?" He stopped what he was doing. "Tom, I just don't know. For myself personally . . . well, I've been happier in this ship than I have ever been before in my life. I've got my wife and kids with me and I'm doing just the work I want to do. With others it may be different."

"How about your kids?"

"Aye, there's the rub. A family man—" He frowned. "I can't advise you, Tom. If I even hint that you should not do what you signed up to do, I'd be inciting to mutiny . . . a capital crime, for both of us. If I tell you that you *must* do what the Captain wants, I'd be on safe legal grounds—but it might mean the death of you and me and my kids and all the rest of us . . . because Chet has horse sense on his side even if the law is against him." He sighed. "Tom, I just missed checking out today—thanks to you—and my judgment isn't back in shape. I can't advise you; I'd be prejudiced."

I didn't answer. I was wishing that Uncle Steve had made it; he always had an answer for everything.

"All I can do," Harry went on, "is to make a weaselly suggestion."

"Huh? What is it?"

"You might go to the Captain privately and tell him just how worried you are. It might affect his decisions. At least he ought to know."

I said I would think about it and thanked him and left. I went to bed and eventually got to sleep. I was awakened in the middle of the night by the ship shaking. The ship always swayed a little when waterborne, but not this way, nor this much, not on Elysia.

It stopped and then it started again . . . and again it stopped . . . and started. I was wondering what . . . when it suddenly quivered in an entirely different way, one that I recognized; it was the way the torch felt when it was just barely critical. The engineers called it "clearing her throat" and was a regular part of overhaul and inspection. I decided that Mr. Regato must be working late, and I quieted down again. The bumping did not start up again.

At breakfast I found out what it was: the behemoths had tried something, nobody knew what, against the ship itself . . . whereupon the Captain had quite logically ordered Mr. Regato to use the torch against them. Now, although we still did not know much about them, we did know one thing: they were not immune to super-heated steam and intense radioactivity.

This brush with the sea devils braced my spine; I decided to see the Captain as Harry had suggested.

He let me in without keeping me waiting more than five minutes. Then he kept quiet and let me talk as long as I wanted to. I elaborated the whole picture, as I saw it, without attributing anything to Chet or Harry. I couldn't tell from his face whether I was reaching him or not, so I put it strongly: that Unc and Mei-Ling were both out of the picture and that the chance that I would be of any use after the next peak was so slight that he was risking his ship and his crew on very long odds.

When I finished I still didn't know, nor did he make a direct answer. Instead he said, "Bartlett, for fifty-five minutes yesterday evening you had two other members of the crew in your room with your door closed."

"Huh? Yes, sir."

"Did you speak to them of this?"

I wanted to lie. "Uh . . . yes, sir."

"After that you looked up another member of the crew and remained with him until quite late . . . or quite early, I should say. Did you speak to him on the same subject?"

"Yes, sir."

"Very well. I am holding you for investigation on two counts: suspicion of inciting to mutiny and suspicion of intent to mutiny. You are under arrest. Go to your room and remain there. No visitors."

I gulped. Then something Uncle Steve had told me came to my aid—Uncle had been a jawbone space-lawyer and loved to talk about it. "Aye, aye, sir. But I insist that I be allowed to see counsel of my choice . . . and that I be given a public hearing."

The Captain nodded as if I had told him that it was raining. "Certainly. Your legal rights will be respected. But those matters will have to wait; we are now preparing to get underway. So place yourself under arrest and get to your quarters."

He turned away and left me to confine myself. He didn't even seem angry.

So here I sit, alone in my room. I had to tell Unc he couldn't come in and, later, Chet. I can't believe what has happened to me.

XVI "JUST A MATHEMATICAL ABSTRACTION"

That morning seemed a million years long. Vicky checked with me at the usual time, but I told her that the watch list was being switched around again and that I would get in touch with her later. *"Is something wrong?"* she asked.

"No, hon, we're just having a little reorganization aboard ship."

"All right. But you sound worried."

I not only didn't tell her that I was in a jam, I didn't tell her anything about the disaster. Time enough later, after it had aged—unless she found out from official news. Meanwhile there was no reason to get a nice kid upset over something she couldn't help.

Twenty minutes later Mr. Eastman showed up. I answered the door when he knocked and told him, "I'm not to have any visitors. Sorry."

He didn't leave. "I'm not a visitor, Tom; I'm here officially, for the Captain."

"Oh." I let him in.

He had a tool kit with him. He set it down and said, "The regular and special communication departments have been consolidated, now that we are so shorthanded, so it looks like I'm your boss. It won't make any difference, I'm sure. But I'm to make a reconnection on your recorder, so that you can record directly into the comm office."

"Okay. But why?"

He seemed embarrassed. "Well . . . you were due to go on watch a half hour ago. We're going to fix this so that you can stand your watches conveniently from here. The Captain is annoyed that I didn't arrange it earlier." He started unscrewing the access plate to the recorder.

I was speechless. Then I remembered something Uncle Steve had told me. "Hey, wait a minute!"

"Eh?"

"Oh, go ahead and rewire it, I don't care. But I won't stand any watches."

He straightened up and looked worried. "Don't talk like that, Tom. You're in enough trouble now; don't make it worse. Let's pretend you never said it. Okay?"

Mr. Eastman was a decent sort and the only one of the electronics people who had never called us freaks. I think he was really concerned about me. But I said, "I don't see how it can be worse. You tell the Captain that I said he could take his watches and—" I stopped. That wasn't what Uncle Steve would say. "Sorry. Please tell him this: 'Communicator Barlett's respects to the Captain and he regrets that he cannot perform duty while under arrest.' Got it?"

"Now look here, Tom, that's not the proper attitude. Surely, there is something in what you say from a standpoint of regulations. But we are shorthanded; everybody has to pitch in and help. You can't stand on the letter of the law; it isn't fair to the rest."

"Can't I?" I was breathing hard and exulting in the chance to hit back. "The Captain can't have his cake and eat it too. A man under arrest doesn't perform duty. It's always been that way and it always will be. You just tell him what I said."

He silently finished the reconnection with quick precision. "You're sure that's what you want me to tell him?"

"Quite sure."

"All right. Hooked the way that thing is now"—he added pointing a thumb at the recorder—"you can reach me or it if you change your mind. So long."

"One more thing—"

"Eh?"

"Maybe the Captain hasn't thought about it, since hi

cabin has a bathroom, but I've been in here some hours. Who takes me down the passageway and when? Even a prisoner is entitled to regular policing."

"Oh. I guess I do. Come along."

That was the high point of the morning. I expected Captain Urqhardt to show up five minutes after Mr. Eastman had left me at my room—breathing fire and spitting cinders. So I rehearsed a couple of speeches in my head, carefully phrased to keep me inside the law and quite respectful. I knew I had him.

But nothing happened. The Captain did not show up; nobody showed up. It got to be close to noon. When no word was passed about standing by for boost, I got in my bunk with five minutes to spare and waited.

It was a long five minutes.

About a quarter past twelve I gave up and got up. No lunch either. I heard the gong at twelve-thirty, but still nothing and nobody. I finally decided that I would skip one meal before I complained, because I didn't want to give him the chance to change the subject by pointing out that I had broken arrest. It occurred to me that I could call Unc and tell him about the failure in the beans department, then I decided that the longer I waited, the more wrong the Captain would be.

About an hour after everybody else had finished eating Mr. Krishnamurti showed up with a tray. The fact that he brought it himself instead of sending whoever had pantry duty convinced me that I must be a Very Important Prisoner —particularly as Kris was unanxious to talk to me and even seemed scared of being near me. He just shoved it in and said, "Put it in the passageway when you are through."

"Thanks, Kris."

But buried in the food on the tray was a note: "Bully for you! Don't weaken and we'll trim this bird's wings. Everybody is pulling for you." It was unsigned and I did not recognize the handwriting. It wasn't Krishnamurti's; I knew his from the time when I was fouling up his farm. Nor was it either of the Travers's, and certainly not Harry's.

167

Finally I decided that I didn't want to guess whose it was and tore it in pieces and chewed it up, just like the Man in the Iron Mask or the Count of Monte Cristo. I don't really qualify as a romantic hero, however, as I didn't swallow it; I just chewed it up and spat it out. But I made darn sure that note was destroyed, for I not only did not want to know who had sent it, I didn't want anybody ever to know.

Know why? That note didn't make me feel good; it worried me. Oh, for two minutes it bucked me up; I felt larger than life, the champion of the downtrodden.

Then I realized what the note meant . . .

Mutiny.

It's the ugliest word in space. Any other disaster is better.

One of the first things Uncle Steve had told me—told Pat and myself, way back when we were kids—was: "The Captain is right even when he is wrong." It was years before I understood it; you have to live in a ship to know why it is true. And I didn't understand it in my heart until I read that encouraging note and realized that somebody was seriously thinking of bucking the Captain's authority . . . and that I was the symbol of their resistance.

A ship is not just a little world; it is more like a human body. You can't have democracy in it, not democratic consent at least, no matter how pleasant and democratic the Captain's manner may be. If you're in a pinch, you don't take a vote from your arms and legs and stomach and gizzard and find out what the majority wants. Darn well you don't! Your brain makes a decision and your whole being carries it out.

A ship in space is like that all the time and has to be. What Uncle Steve meant was that the Captain had better be right, you had better pray that he is right even if you disagree with him . . . because it won't save the ship to be right yourself if he is wrong.

But a ship is not a human body; it is people working together with a degree of selflessness that doesn't come easy—not to me, at least. The only thing that holds it together is misty something called its morale, something you hardly know it has until the ship loses it. I realized then that the *Elsie* had been losing hers for some time. First Doc Devereaux had died and then Mama O'Toole and both of those were body blows. Now we had lost the Captain and most of the rest . . . and the *Elsie* was falling to pieces.

Maybe the new captain wasn't too bright, but he was trying to stop it. I began to realize that it wasn't just machinery breaking down or attacks from hostile natives that lost ships; maybe the worst hazard was some bright young idiot deciding that he was smarter than the Captain and convincing enough others that he was right. I wondered how many of the eight ships that were out of contact had died proving that their captains were wrong and that somebody like me was right.

It wasn't nearly enough to be right.

I got so upset that I thought about going to the Captain and telling him I was wrong and what could I do to help? Then I realized that I couldn't do that, either. He had told me to stay in my room—no 'if's' or 'maybe's.' If it was more important to back up the Captain and respect his authority than anything else, then the only thing was to do as I had been ordered and sit tight.

So I did.

Kris brought me dinner, almost on time. Late that evening the speakers blared the usual warning, I lay down and the *Elsie* boosted off Elysia. But we didn't go on, we dropped into an orbit, for we went into free fall right afterwards. I spent a restless night; I don't sleep well when I'm weightless.

I was awakened by the ship going into light boost, about a half gravity. Kris brought me breakfast but I didn't ask what was going on and he didn't offer to tell me. About the middle of the morning the ship's system called out: "Communicator Bartlett, report to the Captain." It was repeated before I realized it meant me . . . then I jumped up, ran my shaver over my face, decided that my uniform would have to do, and hurried up to the cabin.

He looked up when I reported my presence. "Oh, yes. Bartlett. Upon investigation I find that there is no reason to prefer charges. You are released from arrest and restored to duty. See. Mr. Eastman."

He looked back at his desk and I got sore. I had been seesawing between a feeling of consecrated loyalty to the ship and to the Captain as the head thereof, and an equally strong desire to kick Urqhardt in the stomach. One kind word from him and I think I would have been his boy, come what may. As it was, I was sore.

"Captain!"

He looked up. "Yes?"

"I think you owe me an apology."

"You do? I do not think so. I acted in the interest of the whole ship. However, I harbor no ill feelings, if that is of any interest to you." He looked back at his work, dismissing me . . . as if *my* hard feelings, if any, were of no possible importance.

So I got out and reported to Mr. Eastman. There didn't seem to be anything else to do.

Mei-Ling was in the comm office, sending code groups. She glanced up and I noticed that she looked tired. Mr. Eastman said, "Hello, Tom. I'm glad you're here; we need you. Will you raise your telepartner, please?"

One good thing about having a telepath run the special watch list is that other people don't seem to realize that the other end of each pair—the Earthside partner—is not a disembodied spirit. They eat and sleep and work and raise families, and they can't be on call whenever somebody decides to send a message. "Is it an emergency?" I asked, glancing at the Greenwich and then at the ship's clock. Vicky wouldn't check with me for another half hour; she might be at home and free, or she might not be.

"Perhaps not 'emergency' but 'urgent' certainly."

So I called Vicky and she said she did not mind. ("Code groups, Freckle Face,") I told her. ("So set your recorder on 'play back.' ")

"It's quivering, Uncle Tom. Agitate at will."

For three hours we sent code groups, than which there is nothing more tedious. I assumed that it was probably Captain Urqhardt's report of what had happened to us on Elysia, or more likely his second report after the LRF had jumped him for more details. There was no reason to code it so far as I was concerned; I had been there—so it must be to keep it from our telepartners until LRF decided to release it. This suited me as I would not have relished passing all that blood and slaughter, in clear language, to little Vicky.

While we were working the Captain came in and sat down with Mr. Eastman; I could see that they were cooking up more code groups; the Captain was dictating and Eastman was working the encoding machine. Mei-Ling had long since gone. Finally Vicky said faintly, *"Uncle Tom, how urgent are these anagrams? Mother called me to dinner half an hour ago."*

("Hang on and I'll find out.") I turned to the Captain and Mr. Eastman, not sure of which one to ask. But I caught Eastman's eye and said, "Mr. Eastman, how rush is this stuff? We want to—"

"Don't interrupt us," the Captain cut in. "Just keep on transmitting. The priority is not your concern."

"Captain, you don't understand; I'm not speaking for myself. I was about to say—"

"Carry on with your work."

I said to Vicky, ("Hold on a moment, hon.") Then I sat back and said, "Aye aye, Captain. I'm perfectly willing to keep on spelling eye charts all night. But there is nobody at the other end."

"What do you mean?"

"I mean it is dinner time and way past for my partner. If you want special duty at the Earthside end, you'd better coordinate with the LRF comm office. Seems to me that somebody has the watch list all mixed up."

"I see." As usual he showed no expression. I was beginning to think he was all robot, with wires instead of veins. "Very well, Mr. Eastman, get Mr. McNeil and have him relieve Mr. Bartlett."

"Yes, Captain."

"Excuse me, Captain . . ."

"Yes, Bartlett?"

TIME FOR THE STARS

"Possibly you don't know that Unc's partner lives in Greenwich zone minus-two. It's the middle of the night there—and she is an old lady, past seventy-five. I thought maybe you would want to know."

"Mmm, is that right, Eastman?"

"I believe so, sir."

"Cancel that last order. Bartlett, is your partner willing to go on again after an hour's break for chow? Without clearing it with LRF?"

"I'll see, sir." I spoke to Vicky; she hesitated. I said, ("What is it, Freckle Face? A date with George? Say the word and I'll tell Captain Bligh he can't have you.")

"Oh, it's all right. I'll throw the switch on George. I just wish they would give us something besides alphabet soup. Okay, one hour."

("One hour, sugar plum. Run and eat your salad. Mind your waistline.")

"My waistline is just fine, thank you."

"Okay, Captain."

"Very well. Please thank him for me."

He was so indifferent about it that I added a touch of my own. "My partner is a girl, Captain, not a 'him.' Her mother has placed a two-hour curfew on it. Otherwise it must be arranged with LRF."

"So. Very well." He turned to Eastman. "Can't we manage to coordinate these communication watches?"

"I'm trying, Captain. But it is new to me . . . and we have only three watchstanders left."

"A watch in three should not be too difficult. Yet there always seems to be some reason why we can't transmit. Comment?"

"Well, sir, you saw the difficulty just now. It's a matter of coordinating with Earth. Uh, I believe the special communicators usually arranged that themselves. Or one of them did."

"Which one? Mr. McNeil?"

"I believe Bartlett usually handled it, sir."

"So. Bartlett?"

"I did, sir."

"Very well, you have the job again. Arrange a continuous watch." He started to get up.

How do you tell the Captain he can't have his bucket of paint? "Aye aye, sir. But just a minute, Captain—"

"Yes?"

"Do I understand you are authorizing me to arrange a continuous watch with LRF? Signed with your release number?"

"Naturally."

"Well, what do I do if they won't agree to such long hours for the old lady? Ask for still longer hours for the other two? In the case of my partner, you'll run into parent trouble; she's a young girl."

"So. I can't see why the home office hired such people."

I didn't say anything. If he didn't know that you don't hire telepaths the way you hire butchers, I wasn't going to explain.

But he persisted. "Comment?"

"I have no comment, sir. You can't get more than three or four hours a day out of any of them, except in extreme emergency. Is this one? If it is, I can arrange it without bothering the home office."

He did not answer directly. Instead he said, "Arrange the best watch list you can. Consult with Mr. Eastman." As he turned to leave I caught a look of unutterable weariness on his face and suddenly felt sorry for him. At least I didn't want to swap jobs with him.

Vicky took a trick in the middle of the night, over Kathleen's objections. Kathleen wanted to take it herself, but the truth was that she and I could no longer work easily without Vicky in the circuit, at least not anything as difficult as code groups.

The Captain did not come in to breakfast and I got there late. I looked around and found a place by Janet Meers. We no longer sat by departments—just one big horseshoe table, with the rest of the mess room arranged to look like a lounge, so that it would not seem so empty.

I was just digging into scrambled yeast on toast when Mr. Eastman stood up and tapped a glass for attention. He looked as if he had not slept for days. "Quiet, please. I have a message from the Captain." He pulled out a sheet and started to read:

" 'Notice to All Hands: By direction of the Long Range Foundation the mission of this ship has been modified. We will remain in the neighborhood of Beta Ceti pending rendezvous with Foundation Ship *Serendipity*. Rendezvous is expected in approximately one month. Immediately thereafter we will shape orbit for Earth.

" 'F. X. Urqhardt, commanding *Lewis and Clark*.' "

My jaw dropped. Why, the silent creeper! All the time I had been lambasting him in my mind he had been arguing the home office into canceling our orders . . . no wonder he had used code; you say in clear language that your ship is a mess and your crew has gone to pot. Not if you can help it, you don't. I didn't even resent that he had not trusted us freaks to respect the security of communications; I wouldn't have trusted myself, under the circumstances.

Janet's eyes were shining . . . like a woman in love, or like a relativistic mathematician who has just found a new way to work a transformation. "So they've done it!" she said in a hushed voice.

"Done what?" I asked. She was certainly taking it in a big way; I hadn't realized she was that anxious to get home.

"Tommie, don't you *see?* They've done it, they've done it, they've applied irrelevance. Dr. Babcock was right."

"Huh?"

"Why, it's perfectly plain. What kind of a ship can get here in a month? An *irrelevant* ship, of course. One that is faster than light." She frowned. "But I don't see why it should take even a month. It shouldn't take any time at all. It wouldn't use time."

I said, "Take it easy, Janet. I'm stupid this morning—I didn't have much sleep last night. Why do you say that ship . . . uh, the *Serendipity* . . . is faster than light? That's impossible."

"Tommie, Tommie . . . look, dear, if it was an ordinary ship, in order to rendezvous with us here, it would have had to have left Earth over sixty-three years ago."

"Well, maybe it did."

"Tommie! It couldn't possibly—because that long ago nobody knew that we would be here now. How could they?"

I figured back. Sixty-three Greenwich years ago . . . mmm, that would have been sometime during our first peak. Janet seemed to be right; only an incredible optimist or a fortune teller would have sent a ship from Earth at that time to meet us here now. "I don't understand it."

"Don't you see, Tommie? I've explained it to you, I know I have. Irrelevance. Why, you telepaths were the reason the investigation started; you proved that "simultaneity' was an admissible concept . . . and the inevitable logical consequence was that time and space do not exist."

I felt my head begin to ache. "They don't? Then what is that we seem to be having breakfast in?"

"Just a mathematical abstraction, dear. Nothing more." She smiled and looked motherly. "Poor 'Sentimental Tommie.' You worry too much."

I suppose Janet was right, for we made rendezvous with F. S. *Serendipity* twenty-nine Greenwich days later. We spent the time moseying out at a half gravity to a locus five billion miles Galactic-north of Beta Ceti, for it appeared that the *Sarah* did not want to come too close to the big star. Still, at sixty-three light-years, five billion miles is close shooting—a *very* near miss. We also spent the time working like mischief to arrange and prepare specimens and in collating data. Besides that, Captain Urqhardt suddenly discovered, now that we were expecting visitors, that lots and lots of things had not been cleaned and polished lately. He even inspected staterooms, which I thought was snoopy.

The *Sarah* had a mind reader aboard, which helped when it came time to close rendezvous. She missed us by nearly two light-hours; then their m-r and myself exchanged coordinates (referred to Beta Ceti) by relay back Earthside and got each other pinpointed in a hurry. By radar and radio alone we could have fiddled around for a week—if we had ever made contact at all.

But once that was done, the *Sarah* turned out to be a fast ship, lively enough to bug your eyes out. She was in our lap, showing on our short-range radar, as I was reporting the co-ordinates she had just had to the Captain. An hour later she was made fast and sealed to our lock. And she was a *little* ship. The *Elsie* had seemed huge when I first joined her; then after a while she was just the right size, or a little cramped for some purposes. But the *Sarah* wouldn't have made a decent Earth-Moon shuttle.

Mr. Whipple came aboard first. He was an incredible character to find in space; he even carried a briefcase. But he took charge at once. He had two men with him and they got busy in a small compartment in the cargo deck. They knew just what compartment they wanted; we had to clear potatoes out of it in a hurry. They worked in there half a day, installing something they called a "null-field generator," working in odd clothes made entirely of hair-fine wires, which covered them like mummies. Mr. Whipple stayed in the door, watching while they worked and smoking a cigar —it was the first I had seen in three years and the smell of it made me ill. The relativists stuck close to him, exchanging excited comments, and so did the engineers, except that they looked baffled and slightly disgusted. I heard Mr. Regato say, "Maybe so. But a torch is reliable. You can depend on a torch."

Captain Urqhardt watched it all, Old Stone Face in person.

At last Mr. Whipple put out his cigar and said, "Well, that's that, Captain. Thompson will stay and take you in and Bjorkensen will go on in the *Sarah*. I'm afraid you will have to put up with me, too, for I am going back with you."

Captain Urqhardt's face was a gray-white. "Do I understand, sir, that you are relieving me of my command?"

"What? Good heavens, Captain, what makes you say that?"

"You seem to have taken charge of my ship . . . on behalf of the home office. And now you tell me that this man . . . er, Thompson—will take us in."

"Gracious, no. I'm sorry. I'm not used to the niceties of field work; I've been in the home office too long. But just think of Thompson as a . . . mmm, a sailing master for you. That's it; he'll be your pilot. But no one is displacing you; you'll remain in command until you can return home and turn over your ship. Then she'll be scrapped, of course."

Mr. Regato said in a queer, high voice, "Did you say 'scrapped,' Mr. Whipple?" I felt my stomach give a twist. Scrap the *Elsie*? No!

"Eh? I spoke hastily. Nothing has been decided. Possibly she will be kept as a museum. In fact, that is a good idea." He took out a notebook and wrote in it. He put it away and said, "And now, Captain, if you will, I'd like to speak to all your people. There isn't much time."

Captain Urqhardt silently led him back to the mess deck.

When we were assembled, Mr. Whipple smiled and said, "I'm not much at speechmaking. I simply want to thank you all, on behalf of the Foundation, and explain what we are doing. I won't go into detail, as I am not a scientist; I am an administrator, busy with the liquidation of Project Lebensraum, of which you are part. Such salvage and rescue operations as this are necessary; nevertheless, the Foundation is anxious to free the *Serendipity*, and her sister ships, the *Irrelevant*, the *Infinity*, and *Zero*, for their proper work, that is to say, their survey of stars in the surrounding space."

Somebody gasped. "But that's what *we* were doing!"

"Yes, yes, of course. But times change. One of the null-field ships can visit more stars in a year than a torchship can visit in a century. You'll be happy to know that the *Zero* working alone has located seven Earth-type planets this past month."

It didn't make me happy.

Uncle Alfred McNeil leaned forward and said in a soft, tragic voice that spoke for all of us, "Just a moment, sir. Are you telling us that what we did . . . *wasn't necessary?*"

Mr. Whipple looked startled. "No, no, no! I'm terribly sorry if I gave that impression. What you did was utterly necessary, or there would not be any null ships today. Why, that's like saying that what Columbus did wasn't necessary, simply because we jump across oceans as if they were mud puddles nowadays."

"Thank you, sir," Unc said quietly.

"Perhaps no one has told you just how indispensably necessary Project Lebensraum has been. Very possibly—things have been in a turmoil around the Foundation for some time —I know I've had so little sleep myself that I don't know what I've done and left undone. But you realize, don't you, that without the telepaths among you, all this progress would not have taken place?" Whipple looked around. "Who are they? I'd like to shake hands with them. In any case—I'm not a scientist, mind you; I'm a lawyer—in any case, if we had not had it proved beyond doubt that telepathy is truly instantaneous, proof measured over many light-years, our scientists might still be looking for errors in the sixth decimal place and maintaining that telepathic signals do not propagate instantaneously but simply at a speed so great that its exact order was concealed by instrumental error. So I understand, so I am told. So you see, your great work has produced wondrous results, much greater than expected, even if they are not quite the results you were looking for."

I was thinking that if they had told us just a few days sooner, Uncle Steve would still be alive.

But he never did want to die in bed.

"But the fruition of your efforts," Whipple went on, "did not show at once. Like so many things in science, the new idea had to grow for a long time, among specialists . . . then the stupendous results burst suddenly on the world. For myself, if anyone had told me six months ago that I would be out here among the stars today, giving a popular lecture on the new physics, I wouldn't have believed him. I'm not sure that I believe it now. But here I am. Among other things, I am here to help you get straightened away when we get back home." He smiled and bowed.

"Uh, Mr. Whipple," Chet Travers asked, "just when will we get home?"

"Oh, didn't I tell you? Almost immediately . . . say soon after lunch."

XVII   OF TIME AND CHANGE

I might as well finish this off and give it a decent burial. I'll never have time to write again.

They held us in quarantine for a week at Rio. If it had not been for the LRF man with us, they might have been holding us yet. But they were nice to us. Emperor Dom Pedro III of Brazil presented us each with the Richardson Medal on behalf of the United System and made a speech which showed that he was not quite sure who we were or where we had been, but nevertheless our services were appreciated.

But not as much attention was paid to us as I had expected. Oh, I don't mean that the news services ignored us; they did take our pictures and they interviewed each of us. But the only news story I saw was headed: THIRD LOAD OF RIP VAN WINKLES ARRIVE TODAY.

The reporter or whoever it was who wrote the piece had fun with it and I hope he chokes. It seems that our clothes were quaint and our speech was quaint and we were all deliciously old-fashioned and a bit simple-minded. The picture was captioned: "Off Hats, Chuckies! Grandpa Town-comes."

I didn't look at the stories.

It didn't worry Unc; I doubt if he noticed. He was simply eager to see Celestine. "I do hope," he said to me half seriously, "that child can cook the way her mother could."

"You'll be living with her?" I asked.

"Of course. Haven't we always?"

That was so logical that I had no answer. Then we exchanged addresses. That was logical, too, but it seemed odd —all the address any of us had had was the *Elsie*. But I exchanged addresses with everybody and made a note to look up Dusty's twin, if he was still alive, and tell him he could be proud of his brother—perhaps I could locate him through the Foundation.

When they turned us loose and Celestine Johnson did show up I did not recognize her. I saw this tall, handsome old lady rush up and put her arms around Unc, almost lifting him off his feet, and I wondered if I should rescue him.

But then she looked up and caught my eye and smiled and I yelled, "Sugar Pie!"

She smiled still more and I felt myself washed through with sweetness and love. *"Hello, Tommie. It's good to see you again."*

Presently I promised to visit them at my very first chance and left them; they didn't need me for their homecoming. Nobody had come to meet me; Pat was too old and no longer traveled, Vicky was too young to be allowed to travel alone, and as for Molly and Kathleen, I think their husbands didn't see any reason for it. Neither of them liked me, anyhow. I don't blame them, under the circumstances . . . even though it had been a long time (years to them) since I had mind-talked to their wives other than with Vicky's help. But I repeat, I don't blame them. If telepathy ever becomes common, such things could cause a lot of family friction.

Besides, I was in touch with Vicky whenever I wanted to be. I told her to forget it and not make a fuss; I preferred not to be met.

In fact, save for Unc, almost none of us was met other than by agents of LRF. After more than seventy-one years there was simply no one to meet them. But Captain Urqhardt was the one I felt sorriest for. I saw him standing alone while we were all waiting outside quarantine for our courier-interpreters. None of the rest was alone; we were busy, saying good-by. But he didn't have any friends—I suppose he couldn't afford to have any friends aboard ship, even while he was waiting to become Captain.

He looked so bleak and lonely and unhappy that I walked

up and stuck out my hand. "I want to say good-by, Captain. It's been an honor to serve with you . . . and a pleasure." The last was not a lie; right then I meant it.

He looked surprised, then his face broke into a grin that I thought would crack it; his face wasn't used to it. He grabbed my hand and said, "It's been my pleasure, too, Bartlett. I wish you all the luck in the world. Er . . . what are your plans?"

He said it eagerly and I suddenly realized he wanted to chat, just to visit. "I don't have any firm plans, Captain. I'm going home first, then I suppose I'll go to school. I want to go to college, but I suppose I'll have some catching up to do. There have been some changes."

"Yes, there have been changes," he agreed solemnly. "We'll all have catching up to do."

"Uh, what are your plans, sir?"

"I don't have any. I don't know what I can do."

He said it simply, a statement of fact; with sudden warm pity I realized that it was true. He was a torchship captain, as specialized a job as ever existed . . . and now there were no more torchships. It was as if Columbus had come back from his first voyage and found nothing but steamships. Could he go to sea again? He wouldn't even have been able to find the bridge, much less know what to do when he got there.

There was no place for Captain Urqhardt; he was an anachronism. One testimonial dinner and then thank you, good night.

"I suppose I could retire," he went on, looking away. "I've been figuring my back pay and it comes to a preposterous sum."

"I suppose it would, sir." I hadn't figured my pay; Pat had collected it for me.

"Confound it, Bartlett! I'm too young to retire."

I looked at him. I had never thought of him as especially old and he was not, not compared with the Captain—with Captain Swenson. But I decided that he must be around forty, ship's time. "Say, Captain, why don't you go back to school, too? You can afford it."

He looked unhappy. "Perhaps I should. I suppose I ought to. Or maybe I should just chuck it and emigrate. They say there are a lot of places to choose from now."

"I'll probably do that myself, eventually. If you ask me, things have become too crowded around here. I've been thinking about Connie, and how pretty Babcock Bay looked." I really had been thinking about it during the week we had spent in quarantine. If Rio was a sample, Earth didn't have room enough to fall down; we were clear down in the Santos District and yet they said it was Rio. "If we went back to Babcock Bay, we'd be the oldest settlers."

"Perhaps I will. Yes, perhaps I will." But he still looked lost.

Our courier-interpreters had instructions to take us all home, or wherever we wanted to go, but I let mine leave once I had my ticket for home. She was awfully nice but she bothered me. She treated me as a cross between grandfather who must be watched over in traffic and a little boy who must be instructed. Not but what I needed instruction.

But once I had clothes that would not be stared at, I wanted to be on my own. She had taught me enough System Speech in a week so that I could get by in simple matters and I hoped that my mistakes would be charged up to a local accent from somewhere. Actually, I found that System Speech, when it wasn't upgained to tears, was just P-L lingo with more corners knocked off and some words added. English, in other words, trimmed and stretched to make a trade lingo.

So I thanked Senhorita Guerra and told her good-by and waved my ticket at a sleepy gatekeeper. He answered in Portuguese and I looked stupid, so he changed it to, "Outdowngo rightwards. Ask from allone." I was on my way.

Somehow everybody in the ship seemed to know that I was a Rip Van Winkle and the hostess insisted on helping me make the change at White Sands. But they were friendly and did not laugh at me. One chap wanted to know about the colony being opened up on Capella VIII and did not understand why I hadn't been there if I had spaced all that time. I tried to explain that Capella was clear across the sky and more than a hundred light-years from where I had been, but I didn't put the idea across.

But I did begin to see why we had not made a big splash in the news. Colony planets were the rage and there was a new one every day, so why should anyone be excited over one that we had found sixty years back? Or even over one just a few months back which did not compare with ones being turned up now? As for starships—see the latest news for current departures.

We were going to be a short paragraph in history and a footnote in science books; there wasn't room for us in the news. I decided that even a footnote averaged well and forgot it.

Instead I started thinking about my re-education which, I was beginning to realize, was going to have to be extensive; the changes had been more than I had bargained for. Take female styles, for example—look, I'm no Puritan, but they didn't dress, if you want to call it that, this way when I was a kid. Girls running around without a thing on their heads, not even on top . . . heads bare-naked, like an animal.

It was a good thing that Dad hadn't lived to see it. He never let our sisters come to the table without a hat, even if Pat and I were the only unmarried males present.

Or take the weather. I had known that LRF was working on it, but I never expected them to get anywhere. Don't people find it a little dull to have it rain only at night? Or take trucks. Of course, all you expect of a truck is that it haul things from here to there. But the lack of wheels does make them look unstable.

I wonder how long it will be before there is not a wheel on Earth?

I had decided that I would just have to get used to it all, when the hostess came by and put something in my lap and when I picked it up, it *spoke* to me. It was just a souvenir of the trip.

Pat's town house was eight times as big as the flat seven of us used to live in; I decided that he had managed to hang onto at least some of the money. His robutler took my cape and boots and ushered me in to see him.

He didn't get up. I wasn't sure he could get up. I had known that he was old, but I hadn't realized that he was *old!* He was—let me see, eighty-nine. Yes, that was right; we had our ninetieth birthday coming up.

I tried to keep it casual. "Hi, Pat."

"Hi, Tom." He touched the arm of his chair and it rolled toward me. "Don't move. Stand there and let me look at you." He looked me up and down, then said wonderingly, "I knew intellectually that you would not have changed with the years. But to see it, to realize it, is quite another thing, eh? 'The Picture of Dorian Gray.' "

His voice was old.

"Where is the family?" I said uncomfortably.

"I've told the girls to wait. I wanted to see my brother alone at first. If you mean Gregory and Hans as well, no doubt you will meet them at dinner tonight. But never mind them, lad; just let me visit with you for a while. It's been a long time." I could see tears, the ready tears of old age, in his eyes and it embarrassed me.

"Yes, I guess it has."

He leaned forward and girpped the arms of his chair. "Tell me just one thing. Was it fun?"

I thought about it. Doc Devereaux . . . Mama O'Toole . . . poor little Pru who had never lived to grow up, not really. Uncle Steve. Then I switched it off and gave him the answer he wanted. "Yes, it was fun, lots of fun."

He sighed. "That's good. I quit regretting years ago. But if it hadn't been fun, it would have been such a terrible waste."

"It was."

"That's all I wanted to hear you say. I'll call the girls down in a moment. Tomorrow I'll show you around the plant and introduce you to the key men. Not that I expect you to take hold right away. Take a long vacation if you like. But not too long, Tom . . . for I guess I'm getting old. I can't look ahead the way I used to."

I suddenly realized that Pat had everything planned out, just as he always had. "Wait a minute, Pat. I'll be pleased to have you show me around your plant—and honored. But don't count on anything. First I'm going to school. After that—well, we'll see."

"Eh? Don't be silly. And don't call it 'my' plant; it's 'Bartlett Brothers, Incorporated.' It always has been. It's your responsibility as much as mine."

"Now, take it easy, Pat. I was just—"

"Quiet!" His voice was thin and shrill but it still had the sound of command. "I won't have any nonsense out of you, young man. You've had your own way and you've been off on a long picnic—I won't criticize how you managed it. That's bygones. But now you must buckle down and assume your responsibilities in the family business." He stopped and breathed heavily, then went on more softly, almost to himself. "I had no sons, I have no grandsons; I've had to carry the burden alone. To have my brother, to have my own brother . . ." His voice faded out.

I went up and took him by the shoulder—then I let go; it felt like match sticks. But I decided that I might as well settle it once and for all; I told myself it would be kinder. "Listen to me, Pat. I don't want to seem ungrateful, but you must get this straight. I'm going to live my own life. Understand me. It might include 'Bartlett Brothers'; it might not. Probably not. But *I* will decide. I'll never be told again."

He brushed it aside. "You don't know your own mind; you're just a boy. Never mind, we'll speak of it tomorrow. Today is a day of gladness."

"No, Pat. I am not a boy, I am a man. You'll have to accept that. I'll make my own mistakes and I'll not be told."

He wouldn't look at me. I insisted, "I mean it, Pat. I mean it so much that if you can't accept it and abide by it, I'm walking out right now. Permanently."

Then he looked up. "You wouldn't do that to me."

"I would."

He searched my eyes. "I believe you would. You always were a mean one. You gave me a lot of trouble."

"I'm still mean . . . if you want to call it that."

"Uh . . . but you wouldn't do it to the girls? Not to little Vicky?"

"I will if you force my hand."

He held my eyes for a second, then his shoulders sagged and he buried his face in his hands. I thought he was going to cry and I felt like a villain, bullying an old man like that. I patted his shoulders, wishing that I had stalled, rather than forcing the issue.

I remembered that this frail old man had risked his health and his sanity to get in touch with me at first peak, and I thought: if he wants it so badly, maybe I should humor him. After all, he did not have long to live.

No!

It wasn't right for one person to impose his will on another, through strength or even through weakness. I was myself . . . and I was going out to the stars again. Suddenly I knew it. Oh, college perhaps, first—but I was going. I owed this old man gratitude . . . but I did not owe him the shape of my life. That was mine.

I took his hand and said, "I'm sorry, Pat."

He said without looking up, "All right, Tom. Have it your own way. I'm glad to have you home anyway . . . on your own terms."

We talked inanities for a few moments, then he had the robutler fetch me coffee—he had milk. At last he said, "I'll call the girls." He touched the arm of his chair, a light glowed and he spoke to it.

Molly came down with Kathleen behind her. I would have known either of them anywhere, though I had never seen them. Molly was a woman in her late sixties, still handsome. Kathleen was fortyish and did not look it—no, she looked her age and wore it regally. Molly stood on tiptoe, holding both my hands, and kissed me. "We're glad you are home, Tommie."

"So we are," Kathleen agreed, and her words echoed in my mind. She kissed me, too, then said just with her voice. "So this is my aged and ageless great-uncle. Tom, you make me wish for a son. You aren't uncle-ish and I'll never call you 'uncle' again."

"Well, I don't feel uncle-ish. Except to Molly, maybe."

Molly looked startled, then giggled like a girl. "All right, Uncle Tom. I'll remember your years . . . and treat you with respect."

"Where's Vicky?"

"I'm here, Uncle Tom. Down in a split."

("Hurry, hon.")

Kathleen looked sharply at me, then let it pass—I'm sure she did not mean to listen. She answered, "Vicky will be down in a moment, Tom. She had to get her face just so. You know how girls are."

I wondered if I did. But Vicky was down, almost at once.

There were no freckles on her face, no braces on her teeth. Her mouth wasn't large; it was simply perfectly right for her. And the carroty hair that had worried her so was a crown of flame.

She did not kiss me; she simply came straight to me as if we had been alone, took my hands and looked up at me.

"Uncle Tom. Tom."

("Freckle Face . . .")

I don't know how long we played statues. Presently she said, *"After we are married, there will be none of this many-light-years-apart stuff . . . Understand me? I go where you go. To Babcock Bay, if that's what you want. But I go."*

("Huh? When did you decide to marry me?")

"You seem to forget that I have been reading your mind since I was a baby—and a lot more thoroughly than you think I have! I'm still doing it."

("But how about George?")

"Nothing about George. He was a mere make-do when I thought you would not be back until I was an old lady. Forget him."

("All right.")

Our "courtship" had lasted all of twenty seconds. Without letting go my hands Vicky spoke aloud. "Tom and I are going downtown and get married. We'd like you all to come along."

So we did.

I saw Pat eyeing me after the ceremony, sizing up the new situation and mulling over how he would use it. But Pat doesn't understand the new setup; if I get bossed, it won't be by him. Vicky says that she will soon have me "ricketty all through." I hope not but I suppose she will. If so, I trust I'll be able to adjust to it . . . I've adjusted to stranger things.

Exciting Space Adventure from DEL REY

LEIGH BRACKETT